Deception

Bill Ward

Copyright © 2015 Bill Ward
All rights reserved.
ISBN-13:
978-1519350527

ISBN-10:
151935052X

It is about time I said thanks to my wonderful partner Anja for all her support and encouragement during the writing of my books. She has to put up with me spending long hours unsociably sat at my computer. She is the first reader of everything I write and her feedback helps make the books a better experience for the readers that follow.

CHAPTER ONE

Fawwaz Al-Hashimi had been well trained in the art of making bombs. The first rule his teacher had taught him was to always have respect for the materials. As his teacher was missing three fingers on one hand, Fawwaz deduced his teacher had learned respect the hard way.

Fawwaz had asked to learn how to make bombs so he could bring the war to the doorstep of his enemies, in the way they had brought death and destruction to his homeland. He had pulled the bodies of his sister and mother from the rubble left by the bombs, dropped by the accursed British and American planes.

They fought like cowards, hiding in the sky, shattering both buildings and lives with their technologically advanced weapons but primitive understanding of ancient civilizations, most of which had existed for thousands of years before Columbus ever set foot on America. They did not understand that at the same time their drones left families torn apart, they turned moderates into fanatics. Now these infidels, who waged indiscriminate war against women and children, would learn what it was like to meet your enemy face-to-face on the ground and pay the price for their criminal acts.

It had been explained to Fawwaz that good a soldier as he was on the battlefield, it was by learning how to make bombs that he could properly revenge his family. He had been a good student. It helped that his mind was focused on the single goal of revenge. He didn't waste time, like some of his fellow students, on playing computer games or listening to music. In the time when he wasn't learning how to make bombs, he was training his mind by reading the Koran.

Neither did he have any wish to take a wife. There were plenty of young girls who wanted to serve the cause in the only way they knew how, by marrying a fighter. He considered girls to be an unnecessary distraction so he declined the many offers of marriage. He was of the opinion, learning how to build bombs and distractions like wives were not good bedfellows.

He was fully committed to a noble war. A wife might make him soft and weaken his resolve.

Sometimes, he lied to himself that when the war was won, he would settle down, take a wife and have children. Everyone was entitled to dream. He understood the reality of his short life would be different. He did not want to leave behind a young widow or father children who would never know their father. He was just turned twenty nine years old and doubted he would see thirty. Fate had decreed he was to be an instrument of his God's vengeance.

He had been the star pupil and made many bombs delivered by others over the preceding twelve months but finally it was his time to strike directly at those he hated. He had been willing to be a martyr and wear the suicide vest so he could inflict the most carnage but it had been forbidden. He had been told he was too valuable. It was imperative he remained free as he would be leading a larger, more important attack, planned for the following month. In fact, there was to be a whole campaign of attacks, which would make the enemy too scared to sleep in their beds at night. The idea filled him with joy.

Fawwaz was proud to have been given such an important role in striking at the heart of his enemy. It was his first time in England and though he had so far seen very little of London, where he was staying, he had no interest in being a tourist. His mind was completely focused on his mission. His success would be measured by the number of dead, which he hoped would run to thousands by the time he was finished.

He liked that he was working alone on this first mission. He didn't particularly care for the company of others in normal circumstances, let alone on an important operation. Too many of the others he had fought alongside, had their heart in the right place but simply lacked the skills required to be most effective. It took more than foolish bravery and being devout to be a great warrior. For an important mission it took careful planning and intelligence to guarantee success.

He had done his homework and was ready to make his enemy start to pay for what they had done. He picked up the rucksack and put it on his back. It was quite heavy but that could not be helped. Two days earlier he had travelled the route and he was confident there would be nothing ruining this glorious day.

He had chosen a point to strike where he believed there were no cameras to record his actions. He did not wish to see his face broadcast on the television the next day, which would make it impossible for him to carry out further attacks. But he also knew there were cameras all over London and some would capture his image.

He was dressed in a grey, hooded top and blue jeans. The top was a size too large and the hood fell forward over his forehead, helping to obscure his face. He was also wearing large glasses to further disguise his features. He doubted even his own mother would be able to recognise him from the grainy images typically obtained from CCTV. He checked in the mirror and was confident there was nothing about the way he looked to attract unwanted attention.

The idea for this first attack was not original but that was not important. He had seen videos on YouTube of the previous year's race. The London Marathon attracted about forty thousand runners and even more spectators would line the route. Fawwaz considered it a perfect target. The runners came from all over the world so his action would receive global news coverage. It was impossible for the police to patrol the whole route and it would be easy to escape in the chaos of the aftermath, lost in the mass of people watching the race.

He had recorded a personal video before he arrived in England, which would be broadcast over the internet if, or more likely when, he was finally killed. It was the only time he would be happy to appear on television. He would look down from above and smile at his fame.

Fawwaz checked the time. He had watched the race start on television, more than an hour ago. He had been pleased to see the streets were so packed with runners and those watching, he expected to achieve heavy casualties. It was time and he could not help the smile that spread across his face as he stepped out of his front door. It was a bright clear day, a good day for doing God's work.

"Allahu akbar," he said quietly, touching the photos of his mother and sister, which were in his inside jacket pocket, close to his heart. *God is truly great to give me this chance for revenge.*

CHAPTER TWO

As Baz arrived at the apartment, where eight months earlier he had first enjoyed sex with Lara, he was in an ebullient mood. He was under no illusions Lara would at first refuse his suggestion of sex but today he had significant information to offer in exchange. A little old fashioned bartering was in order. He was going to dangle a carrot and knowing the woman she was, he believed she would be unable to resist the temptation to ensure he was fully on-board. She did not need to know the truth, which was that he was going to feed her the information whether or not she agreed to sex. He ultimately had no choice in that matter.

Today, he would be putting in motion a plan conceived two years earlier. Baz didn't know why the man he knew only as Phoenix, wanted this information passed to the British but he understood it was of the utmost importance. Baz also knew if Phoenix was made aware of the fact he was bartering with the information for sex, he would not be happy and Phoenix was definitely not a man Baz would wish to make unhappy. Still, life was one eternal risk after another. On the scale of risks he took, the chances of Phoenix finding out about this particular risk were negligible.

Lara arrived punctually as always and Baz hurriedly ushered her into the living room. The anticipation of her arrival had been almost too much to bear.

"It is good to see you, Lara," Baz greeted her with a broad smile.

"You seem in an especially good mood," Lara commented, surprised by the friendly welcome. Over the previous few months of their meeting, she had never previously seen the hint of a smile.

"I am always excited to see you, Lara. Ever since that first memorable time in this apartment."

Lara didn't like Baz referring to the first time they had met when she had sex with him in order to entrap him. He had supplied a steady stream of worthwhile information since then and there had been no question of her having further sex with him. It was in her hands whether he lived or died and she believed that was sufficient incentive for him to double-cross his terrorist friends. One word from her and those same friends would undoubtedly give him a very slow and agonising death.

"So what do you have for me today?" Lara asked, taking a seat at the small table. It was their routine that he would sit opposite her but he made no sign of doing so.

"Would you like something to drink?" Baz asked.

"No thanks, I am in a hurry. I have another meeting after this," she lied.

"You will want to stay longer when you hear what I have to tell you today."

Lara became more attentive. This promise of special information and Baz's happy mood suggested this was not going to be just another routine meeting. "What do you know?" she asked, trying to control her impatience as he turned his back and went to the kettle.

"First, I am going to make some tea and then I am going to enjoy your company. Afterwards, I will give you the information you crave."

"Look Baz, stop messing me about and just tell me what you have to tell me."

"No, Lara. I have been risking my life for a long time, providing you with good information but today is far more important than anything I have previously provided. It is only fair that you reward me for my contribution to a meteoric rise in your career."

"I'm not fucking you," she said flatly, finally understanding where the conversation was going.

"Think of it then as me fucking you." He laughed at his attempt at humour.

"If you don't tell me something soon I'm going to leave here and inform your colleagues how you have been helping us," Lara threatened.

"You won't do that. It is what I believe you English call, cutting off your nose to spite your face. I am too valuable and I don't think your superiors would be very happy with you losing me as a source. Is it not your job to keep me happy?"

Lara felt uncomfortable. He had proved to be valuable and should his information dry up so would her immediate career prospects. She didn't want to have sex with him but she suspected that because he was changing the dynamic of their meeting, he really did have something significant to trade.

"Can you give me everything I need to know within twenty minutes?" she asked.

"That should not be a problem," he confirmed.

"Then you have thirty minutes of my time to do with as you wish but not a minute more. I cannot be late for my next meeting."

"I suppose I have to be grateful for small mercies."

"And this information had better be worth it," she threatened. "Otherwise, I swear you will regret this."

"Trust me, you will not be disappointed. Now I suggest you remove your clothes as we are wasting my valuable time."

Lara quickly undressed and discarded her clothes on the floor. There was no hint of seduction in the way she removed her clothes. She had no intention of being an equal partner in what was about to take place. She wanted him to know she was doing this under duress not for pleasure.

Baz had watched her undress without removing any of his clothes. "You are a beautiful woman," he said, once she was naked. "Lie on the sofa."

She spread herself out on the sofa and watched as he undressed. She remembered clearly Baz's sexual preferences. He liked only anal and oral sex. Everything else was reserved for his wife. The hypocrisy was absurd but she found much about Saudi men to be bizarre.

As he removed his boxers, she wasn't surprised to see he was already erect. She enjoyed the male form and had always been able to divorce the act of sex from love or emotions. The demands of her job had made it necessary but in truth, it hadn't been any great sacrifice learning how to use sex to recruit assets. Men were easily manipulated by their egos and cock.

She opened her legs hoping he would take the invitation but instead he moved to the side of the sofa, level with her face. He directed his cock straight to her face and she took the end in her mouth. Perhaps he would settle for a simple blow job. She started to suck deeper and he placed his hands behind her head, one hand holding on tightly to her hair. As he thrust he pulled her head towards him, forcing himself deeper.

She had her hand around the base of his cock, restricting how deep he could penetrate.

"Hold your hands behind your back," he instructed. "And don't move them."

She did as he asked and interlocked her fingers as she clasped her hands tightly together. She understood what he wanted.

His next thrust found her lips up against his skin and he held her there for several seconds until she could take no more and forced her head back so she could breath. He gave her only a couple of seconds before he again pulled on her head as he thrust and buried himself deep in her throat. He repeated the action several times and with his spare hand reached down and started playing with her nipples.

"Now I'm going to properly fuck your pretty face," he said, suddenly stopping.

He took her under the arms and pulled her to the end of the sofa so her head hung backwards over the arm. He took hold of his cock and slid it into her mouth. Upside down, her throat was more open and he was able to reach even deeper.

Lara believed that each time Baz buried himself in her throat he was repaying her for what she had done to him, turning him into a traitor. It was his small chance for revenge but whatever his motives, she couldn't deny she was now completely aroused and enjoying being submissive to his sexual desires. For a short time at least she could lose control and forget everything except a primeval need.

As he grunted and thrust deep for a final time she swallowed his cum. He stayed in her mouth and squeezed the end of his cock, ensuring she had every last drop. Then he walked away without saying anything.

After a few seconds she sat back up. She reached for her knickers from the floor.

"You won't be needing them," Baz said, from across the room. "I haven't finished with you." He took a large vibrator from the sideboard drawer and held it up for her to see clearly. "I have invested in a new toy for your pleasure. It is larger than my previous one."

"You had your fun," she replied impatiently. "What about this information?"

"You said I could have you for half an hour. I have plenty of time left. You get your information when I've finished with you."

She glanced at her watch, he had about fifteen minutes left. She would quite like to get off as well so decided against arguing but she had no intention of letting him know how she felt. "If you insist," she said, throwing her knickers back on the floor. "How do you want me?"

"Doggy style like the first time."

She glanced at his cock and it was still looking quite stiff. "Have you some lube?" she asked, assuming he would be wanting anal sex. She had recently read that anal sex was forbidden under Islam even between consenting married couples. The punishment in their case would undoubtedly be death. She smiled at the thought. It certainly added a greater sense of danger to having sex than just being caught by your parents when you were a teenager.

"Yes and this is for you." Baz handed over the vibrator. "I remember you enjoyed playing with my toy last time."

Lara took hold of the toy and knelt on the sofa, sticking out her bottom. She felt the trickle of lube running down her backside and shortly afterwards he entered her, slowly at first but then after a couple of seconds he buried himself balls deep and she grimaced.

He thrust deeply and slowly. He didn't rush and seemed intent on enjoying every sensation. She suspected he was again using sex as payback time. She placed the vibrator between her legs and the way it slid so easily inside her body, confirmed her physical need whatever her head might be thinking.

The feeling of both holes filled so tightly took her mind away from any thought except the desire to orgasm. She pushed her hips back to fully receive his cock and he began thrusting quicker. She knew he wouldn't be able to keep it up for long and soon he was grunting and exploding inside her. She had the vibrator on maximum speed and her own orgasm overtook her whole body. She collapsed forward on the sofa as he withdrew.

She didn't like that her body had betrayed her with its automatic responses. She would have liked to stoically take his fucking her without showing any sign of interest but once he started, her body had responded of its own accord and she had wanted, in fact needed, his cock.

Lara knew she had to regain control of the meeting. She stood up, collected her clothes from the floor and walked to the bathroom where she spent two minutes under the hot shower. When she returned to the living room, Baz was sitting at the table drinking tea.

"We must do that more often," he said. "It makes our meetings so much more pleasant."

"Nothing about what we just did was remotely pleasant," she snapped, although in truth her orgasm had told a different story. "And it won't be happening again." In her mind she was wondering if he was going to become a problem at their future meetings.

"It is a small price to pay for the information I provide," Baz said. "And I think you actually found it quite enjoyable."

She sat across the table from Baz and looked him straight in the eyes. "Perhaps I should use the toy on you next time? If you think anal sex is so enjoyable."

"We can discuss it the next time."

She couldn't believe she had been so stupid as to suggest there might be a next time. She needed to get back on track. "It's time for you to live up to your end of the bargain. What do you have for me?"

"A man has recently flown to England. Unfortunately, I did not learn of this until yesterday. I am told this man's presence in the UK is highly significant. He undertakes only the most important operations. I do not know his exact mission but it may even be that he is the one responsible for the bombing of the London Marathon."

"Who is this man?" Lara demanded. The capture of the bomber was the number one priority within all the security services. To deliver the name of the bomber to her bosses would be an amazing addition to her CV.

"Have you made any progress with finding the bomber?" Baz asked, ignoring Lara's question.

In truth, Lara had no idea what progress had been made. She was too far removed from the investigation. "I am not going to share such information with you. Perhaps you are here just to find out what we know about the bomber."

"Lara, you are so distrusting."

"I have to be. I spend my life around people like you."

"Now you have hurt me."

"You'll get over it. So when did this man arrive in England?"

"Recently."

Lara was getting angry. She felt like she was being played for a fool. "You mean to tell me I let you fuck me just so you could tell me some man has already flown to England to do something but you don't know for sure what. You're taking the piss!"

Baz was smiling. "You should not speak like that. It is not ladylike."

"Fuck you!"

"You forget my role in the organisation. I promised important information and I keep my word. I provided the passport for this man to travel. It is not his real name but the passport is in the name of Fawwaz Al-Hashimi."

Lara's heart skipped a beat. There would be a record of this man entering Britain. She needed to urgently return to the embassy and set in motion steps to find him.

"Now I think you are happy with our arrangement," Baz continued.

She had to admit, Baz had delivered on his promise after all. Delivered big time in fact. A fresh thought crossed her mind. "I hope you haven't been sitting on this information waiting until after the bombing before passing me his name. That would be a very dangerous game to play."

"I swear on my children's lives I only learned the significance of this name yesterday."

"Is there anything else you can tell me about this man or his mission? Is he definitely a bomber?" she asked.

"I don't know for certain but I will try to find out more. If I hear anything we can meet again for another pleasant time."

Lara gave him a cold stare. "Don't push me." Then more lightly she added, "Maybe when we have this man in custody we can consider spending some more pleasant time together but until then your cock stays firmly inside your clothes."

She thought there was no harm in offering Baz an extra incentive to help find this man. A promise was all it would ever be.

CHAPTER THREE

The knock at the door brought Fawwaz instantly alert. He was not expecting any visitors. He had been instructed to lie low for a few days and then he would receive further instructions about his next target. In the five days since his bombing of the marathon, he had not left the house.

It was a small terraced property and in need of renovation but Fawwaz didn't care. It served its purpose. There was an adequate kitchen for his simple needs. The bathroom, despite the cracked tiles and some damp causing mildew around the floor, had a good shower. In the mornings, he would spend several minutes under the shower, mixing the temperature from hot to very cold, in order to invigorate his body.

There were stained curtains on the windows, which he kept permanently closed. He didn't want anyone peering inside his workshop because that was how he thought of the house. It was not a home but a place for him to prepare bombs. At the moment though, he had no more materials for bombs and had to wait patiently to be resupplied.

He maintained his fitness by twice a day doing press ups and pulls ups. He would also stand in the middle of the room with his hands outstretched holding the kettle and toaster as weights. He was not truly concerned about losing his fitness in such a short time but exercising helped keep boredom at bay.

There was plenty of food in the house and he spent the vast majority of his time watching television, mostly glued to the BBC and Al Jazeera news channels. He was confident there was no evidence linking him to the explosion. According to the news, the police had no suspects. Certainly they had not broadcast any photos of him so his attempts to avoid cameras seemed to have been successful.

He had been disappointed by his limited success. He had hoped to kill hundreds not just a handful of people. Fortunately, there would be further targets and he was confident of killing far more of the enemy next time. He would not return home until his family were properly avenged. In truth, he knew he would probably never go back but he would make the English pay dearly for their crimes.

There was a second knock at the door. He could pretend he was not at home but if whoever was outside had heard him, then it might attract more attention. The one thing he didn't want was to be noticed. If it was someone come to kill him on the other side of the door, they would not be politely knocking.

He regretted not being properly armed. He felt naked without a gun. He picked up the large kitchen knife from the table and put it through the belt of his jeans and under his shirt so it wasn't visible. He had been wearing European clothing since arriving in the country to help blend in with the locals.

"Good morning," the man on the doorstep said. He was middle aged and dressed casually. His shoulders were hunched and he was clearly no danger. There was a badge pinned to the man's jacket. "I'm here to read the gas meter."

"I was just going out, can you please come back another time?" Fawwaz asked politely. He spoke good English. One hand was behind his back grasping the handle of the knife.

"It will only take a minute. This meter hasn't been read for a very long time."

The man took a pace forward and gave Fawwaz little choice but to let him in. There were people walking by on the street. He couldn't risk trouble.

"Do you know where the meter is?" the man asked.

Fawwaz closed the front door. "I believe it is under the stairs," he said, leading the way to a small cupboard, bending down and opening the double doors.

He was careful to ensure the knife was concealed. As he stood back up, the first thing he noticed was the extended arm and the weapon, then he noticed the man was smiling.

"On the floor," the man commanded. "Get on the floor," he repeated when Fawwaz was slow to move.

Still Fawwaz didn't move. He was calculating the possibility of disarming this man but he was keeping his distance. His body no longer sagged but was upright and the man had an air of confidence, like he had done this before.

"Lie down now or I will put a bullet in your knee," the man threatened, taking a step backwards.

Fawwaz wondered if the man had read his mind. There was too much distance between them. He had no chance of overpowering the man. And if his knee was shattered, there would be no possibility of escape in the future. He wished he had worn a suicide vest at the marathon. He could have died a martyr and killed so many more of the enemy. Fawwaz did as ordered and prostrated himself on the floor.

There was the crashing sound of the front door being taken off its hinges and suddenly the hallway was flooded with people. He felt two burly men pull his hands behind his back and apply handcuffs. He was searched and the knife removed from his belt. Then he was pulled to his feet and a hood put over his head.

Fawwaz felt himself dragged out the front door and seconds later he was being bundled into the back of a van. He had never known such a desperate feeling of misery. He had failed in his mission and he would never be able to fully revenge his family.

CHAPTER FOUR

Powell was sitting, drinking a coffee and reading the newspaper when his phone rang. It was the leisurely way he started most mornings. He glanced to see who was calling and could barely believe the name that appeared. He wasn't sure why her name and number were still in his phone.

"Hello Lara," he answered, tentatively. "This is a surprise. I didn't expect to ever hear from you again."

"Powell, can I come and see you?"

There was an urgency and something else in her voice that made him become alert. She sounded scared. He didn't think of Lara as someone who would scare easily.

"Has something happened?" he probed.

"I can't talk on the phone but I need your help."

Powell realised she must be really desperate if he was the person she was turning to when in need of help. "When do you want to come?"

"How about this afternoon?"

"Are you in England?"

"Yes, I arrived a few days ago."

"Okay. My bar is called Bella's and is in Hove. I'll be here all day. It's a ten minute taxi from Brighton station."

"Thank you. I'll be there about two."

Powell realised she had disconnected before he could ask any further questions. As he put the phone down on the table, he was in a state of shock. He hadn't thought about Lara for many months. She was strictly history and he had never thought he would see her again.

He wondered what had brought her to England and whether it had anything to do with Baz and the children. He hoped not. The children were happy back home with their mother. Lost in his thoughts, he didn't notice Afina approach.

"Are you still okay to look after things tonight?" she asked.

"Of course I am. You know, I did manage to run this bar for twenty years before you arrived." Powell had recently become almost superfluous to running the bar, Afina did such a good job of managing everything. "You and Mara have fun. Who is it you're seeing?"

"Jason Derulo."

"Sorry, never heard of him."

"Want to want me?"

"That sounds confusing."

"It's a song."

"Not ringing any bells. Listen, I'm expecting a visitor about two this afternoon so I'll use the office, if that's okay?"

"Of course, it is your office," Afina replied with a grin.

Powell sensed Afina would like to know more about his visitor but he had no intention of letting her know it was Lara. After coming back from Saudi, Powell had given Afina an edited version of events and mentioned Lara's name but not the fact they had been lovers.

"What time do you plan to get away tonight?" Powell asked, changing the subject.

"Mara's coming over for a drink about six and we'll leave about seven, I guess."

"That's fine with me. Let me finish my coffee and then I'll help you behind the bar a bit. See if I can remind myself how it all works."

"I read once elephants never forget," Afina said.

"That may be true of elephants but I'm more of a dinosaur."

"Must be why you've never heard of Jason Derulo," Afina said, as she walked away.

Powell enjoyed his relationship with Afina. She no longer looked at him with puppy dog eyes and hadn't made any further suggestions they should have a sexual relationship. Not that he was completely averse to the idea. He couldn't deny he found her very attractive and there was no other woman in his life. He had gone back to being celibate. In fact, one of the reasons it would be strange to see Lara again was because she was the last person he had sex with and that was almost a year ago.

He enjoyed the banter he shared with Afina and Mara had even described them as like an old married couple. In private, Mara would ask him when he was going to get together with Afina. Mara would always say they were meant for each other. Sometimes he wasn't sure if she was serious or just desperate to be a bridesmaid, which she had insisted she would be, when they finally tied the knot. In her opinion, he was just delaying the inevitable.

Powell didn't share Mara's view. Afina deserved the chance to have a family, something he was certain he didn't want. He was too old to start changing nappies again and have his nights interrupted by crying babies. He was sure he would make a terrible father second time around.

With Afina it would have to be all or nothing. He couldn't just be her boyfriend for a few years, before inevitably breaking up when her need for children became greater than her need to stay with him. He knew if he opened the door to a relationship with Afina, she would expect marriage, kids, the full works.

Powell recognised Afina put all her energies into her work. He continued to be impressed with how she ran the bar. She went through the motions of asking his opinion from time to time but he knew she did it out of politeness, rather than truly needing his help. As a result, he found himself with far more free time on his hands than had been the case for most of the last twenty years. He was attending kick boxing training three evenings a week and getting back to peak fitness.

Powell hoped Afina would find a boyfriend but there was no sign of anyone. She had been invited out by a few of the customers but she always declined politely. He wasn't surprised given her past experiences. It was going to take someone very special to win Afina's heart.

CHAPTER FIVE

As Powell waited for Lara to arrive, he had an uneasy feeling in his stomach. He was certain Lara wasn't just paying him a social visit but wasn't sure what to expect. Powell had mixed feelings concerning Lara. On the one hand he was intensely attracted to her but he had discovered the hard way, he could never really trust her motives. He didn't want to be drawn into some further web of deceit of her origin.

Life had returned to a more normal existence since his return from Saudi. There was no longer any Romanian gangsters trying to kill him and he was coming to terms with the loss of Bella. He recognised that in some ways, Afina had filled part of the void left by Bella's death. He still had dark moments and on a daily basis he would speak to Bella, share things and ask advice. She was still very much alive in his mind.

Powell was behind the bar when Lara arrived. She was wearing blue jeans, a red jumper and a leather jacket. Her jet black hair framed a naturally suntanned complexion. She looked as stunning as he remembered. She stood at the entrance and looked around until her eyes fell upon Powell. She smiled the same captivating smile he remembered and walked towards him.

"Hello, Lara." He noticed for the first time she had bags under her brown eyes, which hadn't been there the last time they met. She looked tired.

"Powell…" There was a second while they both just studied each other. She took the initiative and kissed him on both cheeks in greeting. "Thanks for seeing me. I wouldn't have been surprised if you'd told me you never wanted to see me again."

"It sounded important."

"It is. Can we sit down and talk?"

"Would you like a drink. Coffee or something stronger? I'm going to have a Latte."

"A double espresso would be good."

"Coming right up." He turned to the coffee machine behind to make the drinks.

"This is a great bar," Lara said, casting her eyes around.

"Thanks."

In the mirror behind the bar, Powell could see Lara checking out the bar. He was fairly sure she was taking more than a casual interest. She was taking note of all the other customers and the layout, in a way he had done twenty years before when he worked for MI5. She was checking entrances and exits.

Powell placed the two coffees on the counter. "Have you eaten? We do good food."

"I'm fine thanks. Let's sit and talk."

"Okay, let's go through to my office."

Before Powell could pick up his coffee he noticed three men enter, cast their eyes around and then head directly in his direction. They all looked like clones with their dark suits, white shirts and short haircuts. They looked as if they were on official business and he had a nasty foreboding they weren't here to eat or drink.

"We have visitors," Powell nodded in the direction of the men as they came near.

Lara gasped as she turned and saw the men. From her reaction, Powell thought she recognised them.

"Can I help you?" Powell asked.

"You need to come with us," the man in the middle of the three said to Lara, completely ignoring Powell. He was slightly shorter than the other two. The men on either side of him were both wearing sun glasses, which seemed decidedly odd given it wasn't the least bit sunny outside.

"What is going on here?" Powell asked more firmly.

"This woman is under arrest," the spokesman responded. "Please step back. She is dangerous."

"Don't let them take me, Powell," Lara pleaded. "They'll make me disappear."

Powell noticed the two men on the side were slowly circling Lara, trapping her against the bar.

"If she's under arrest, show me your identification," Powell demanded.

"Please keep out of this, Sir. It's none of your concern."

"You're not police. You have an American accent and you're friends look like extras from a Men in Black movie."

"Are you going to come quietly?" the American asked, turning back to

Lara. "We don't want any trouble in here. People may get hurt."

"She's going nowhere," Powell stated. "Now get out of my bar."

The two men in sunglasses both grabbed for each of Lara's arms. Powell moved quickly. He grabbed the baseball bat from under the counter and brought it crashing down on the arm of one of the men as he struggled to hold onto Lara's arm. The bat was a new addition to the bar and had been Afina's decision in case of any further trouble from her countrymen.

There was a scream from the man who let go of Lara and backed away holding on to his broken arm. With one arm free, Lara swung a wild punch at the second man holding her other arm. He stepped back and looked to the man without glasses for guidance. The bar wasn't busy but the brief fight had attracted everyone's attention.

Powell held the bat above his shoulder, ready to bring it down again on anyone who encroached within range.

"You will regret this," the American threatened. He half withdrew a gun from inside his jacket so it was visible only to Powell and Lara. The implied threat was obvious. "The girl is coming with us," he said forcibly.

"She's going nowhere," Powell replied evenly. "Our cameras are filming everything. Even you couldn't be stupid enough to use that in front of so many witnesses. I assume whoever you're working for wouldn't be very happy seeing your faces all over the evening news."

Powell saw a moment's indecision in the man's eyes then he turned and walked away, beckoning for the other two to follow.

For the first time, Powell noticed Afina looking at him from a corner table. She looked angrily in his direction. He knew she had worked hard over the last eight months to restore the bar's reputation. He lowered the bat and replaced it under the counter.

"Thank you," Lara said. "I think you might have just saved my life."

"You have a great deal of explaining to do," Powell replied. "Do you know those men?"

"I've seen the one who was doing all the talking before but I've never actually spoken to him."

Out of the corner of his eye, Powell could see Afina going around the tables, no doubt telling the diners there was nothing to worry about. Powell hoped the three men having left was more than just a temporary reprieve for the bar.

"I'm having a proper drink," he announced, deciding to put further questions for Lara on hold until they were alone. He took a bottle of whisky from the side and poured himself a double measure. "What about you?"

"I'll have a glass of white wine, please," Lara replied.

"We need some privacy. Let's go to the office," Powell suggested, pouring a very large glass of wine. He hoped wine might loosen Lara's tongue.

He led the way with Lara following close behind. After closing the door and sitting behind the desk, he came straight to the point. "You've really pissed someone off. What did those men want?"

Before Lara could answer, she was interrupted by the door opening. Afina entered and seeing both chairs occupied she stood leaning against the wall with her arms crossed.

There was something of a pregnant pause then Afina looked at Powell and asked, "Aren't you going to introduce us?"

CHAPTER SIX

Powell had hoped to be able to speak with Lara without Afina present but now she was in the room, he wasn't going to send her away.

"Afina, this is Lara."

Afina gave Lara a cold stare. "You are the Lara from Saudi Arabia?" she asked without disguising her hostility.

Lara seemed taken aback. "I guess I am the same one." She looked at Powell for support.

"Afina is the manager of the bar," Powell explained. "And a very close friend."

It was Lara's turn to stare at Afina. "I'm sorry for what happened. I had no idea they were following me."

"Who are they?" Powell asked again. He could see the girls exchanging looks, assessing each other and he suspected both were wondering if the other had been his lover.

"I really don't know." Lara replied. "They obviously work for a government agency but I couldn't say for sure which agency or for that matter, which government."

"What do they want with you?" Powell asked.

"I don't know."

"You don't seem to know very much," Afina snapped. "I don't care what happens to you but Powell could have been killed."

"Powell, I think we should speak in private," Lara said. "This doesn't concern your friend."

"I'm not sure it concerns me either," Powell answered. Reluctantly he turned to Afina. "Give us some time, please, Afina."

Afina stormed out of the room and slammed the door .

"I think she has strong feelings for you," Lara said. "Isn't she a bit young for you?"

"I love Afina like a daughter, nothing else," Powell stressed.

"I don't think that's how she views you. Have you slept with her?"

Powell was thrown by the question. "Look, we're getting off track. Can we please leave my personal life out of this and get back to what brings you to Brighton."

"Okay. Ten days ago I met with Baz and he gave me the name of an important terrorist who had recently entered the UK. It was a couple of days after the London Marathon."

Powell immediately understood the significance. He had run the marathon a couple of times and was watching the race on the television when the bomb exploded. The explosion at the side of the road would have killed many more people if it hadn't been for the police officer stumbling across the bag and carrying it away from the crowd so he could check inside. Even so, there had been seven deaths, including the policeman and twenty people injured, some seriously.

"Was it him?" Powell asked.

"I immediately passed the information up the line with my recommendation it was reliable and likely to be the same man." Lara paused to take a drink of her wine. "Obviously, our people immediately launched a nationwide search for this man."

"Are they any closer to finding him?" He knew the terrorist was still at large.

"It took them just a few days to locate him."

Powell was shocked. "There's been nothing in the papers about an arrest."

"The decision was taken that he needed to be interrogated without the hindrance of due process. We needed to discover if there were other terrorists planning further bombings."

"Isn't that what the Americans used to do with rendition, when they shipped prisoners out of the country to torture them somewhere that didn't give a damn about human rights?"

Lara took another drink of wine before answering, "Yes."

"Has this terrorist been taken out of the country?"

"No."

Powell realised what he was learning was the type of information that would be highly classified and could be very dangerous knowing. "Where do you fit in all this?" he asked.

"Five days ago I was told to get to Vauxhall urgently to be part of the interrogation team. I had learned a little more about the terrorist from Baz and it was thought my knowledge could prove useful. Some expert thought it would help break him if he realised he had been betrayed and I was the best person to describe the betrayal." She took another large drink of wine before she continued. "Only I never actually made it to Vauxhall. I was met at Heathrow and told there was a change in plans. I was put on a helicopter and flown to a large house somewhere in the country."

Powell raised his eyebrows. "Do you know whereabouts?"

"Not really because I was too busy being briefed. I wasn't paying attention to any landmarks. I remember the journey went quickly, certainly less than thirty minutes. And I think we flew East."

"So probably somewhere in Kent or Essex. What happened when you got there?"

"I've never seen anything like it." Lara's eyes were cast down at the floor. She was obviously deeply disturbed by the memory. "I honestly didn't believe we did such things."

"What things?" Powell prompted gently.

"It doesn't matter but they did things to the terrorist that physically made me sick. And I have a strong stomach."

"You mean they tortured him?"

"Yes. And it was a hundred times worse than Waterboarding."

Powell was shocked and pretty certain such treatment of even a terrorist suspect was always illegal in the UK.. He doubted there were any circumstances in which even Executive Orders from the Prime Minister could grant powers to interrogate by such methods. "Did they get the information they wanted?" he asked.

"Yes. They seemed very happy with the results... Powell, I'll never forget the screams I heard from that man. It was inhuman."

"You said you'd seen the man from the bar before," he prompted, keen to get back to the present. He had only limited sympathy for the terrorist's suffering.

"Yes, he was the man doing most of the torturing. I observed some of the early sessions. Just thinking about him gives me nightmares."

"And why do you think he came here looking for you?"

"I'm not sure," answered Lara and drank more wine. "After they had what they wanted from the terrorist, I was given a helicopter ride back to Battersea. I was told not to breathe a word of what I'd seen, which was rather stating the obvious and as I was on holiday for the next few days, I was told to stay away from Vauxhall. I should return to Saudi after my holiday and continue working as normal."

"So what happened to make you scared and need to pay me a visit?"

"I was stupid. I put an email to my boss in Saudi telling him I didn't like what I had seen and I believed what I had seen was illegal. I asked him what I should do. I had an almost immediate reply telling me to forget what I had seen and just enjoy my holiday. We could talk about it further when I returned to work."

"Probably sound advice."

"Yes but I couldn't leave it alone. What I'd seen had made me angry. It makes us as bad as the terrorists. We can't claim to be the good guys and then inflict the most horrible torture on people. We have to respect the legal process. I was determined not to let it drop and I felt I should speak to someone at Vauxhall, while I was still in the country. In the end, my boss persuaded me to leave it with him for a couple of days and he'd make some enquiries..."

Powell thought Lara had acted very naively but he couldn't criticise her motives. Perhaps she wasn't quite such a manipulative and cynical bitch as she had portrayed in Saudi. "Have you heard back from him?"

"No, that was two days ago. Ever since I've been followed and yesterday I'm convinced they tried to kill me."

"What happened?"

"I've been staying with my father in Dulwich. I popped out yesterday morning to do a bit of shopping and a car tried to run me over. Luckily I have fast reactions and I'm fit so I managed to jump out of the way at the last second. I just ended up with some bruises."

"Perhaps it was just a drunk or someone on a mobile who didn't see you."

"The car swerved towards me and he didn't stop. He knew what he was doing," she said with absolute conviction. "I remembered you had a friend in MI5 so that's when I decided to pay you a visit. I knew I was being followed again this morning but I thought I'd got rid of them before I took the train here. I'm sorry, I shouldn't have involved you in this."

"Shouldn't you speak with your boss in Saudi and see if he can help?"

"It's only since I spoke with him last time that I'm in this mess. I don't trust him."

Powell was thoughtful for a moment. "The three men could have been just a precaution. They may have wanted to remind you of having signed The Official Secrets Act and warn you they could throw you in jail if you spoke about what you'd seen."

"Maybe but that doesn't explain the car yesterday. If I had reacted a fraction slower I wouldn't be here now. And if they can do what I saw to that terrorist, then they obviously don't care about the law. They might have decided it's easier not to take the risk I might speak about what I saw and silence me permanently."

"Do you know what information they extracted from the terrorist?"

"Details of a planned attack next month and the names of a couple of terrorists in Bradford, who were to be part of the attack."

"What was the target?"

"Suffice to say it was a large scale bombing aimed at the heart of government. I actually take having signed The Official Secrets Act very seriously… I'm worried now I've put you in danger."

"I need to speak with my friend and see what I can find out. By the way, isn't it odd that man had an American accent?"

"We work closely with the Americans on all terrorist matters. He could be on secondment to us. Perhaps he was brought in specifically to lead the interrogation. I'm pretty sure he had questioned people before using the same methods. He… "

"What?"

"He seemed to enjoy what he was doing."

Powell was willing to believe the Americans would have people with specialist skills in interviewing terrorist suspects, otherwise why bother to have a programme of rendition. But it wasn't something they would want publicised any more than the UK government would want it known they had used such a man or his methods, to gain information. Powell was becoming more concerned, the more he heard.

"You better stay with me for the time being," Powell suggested and saw the look of relief on Lara's face. He wished Lara had never walked into his bar but he couldn't just send her away when her life was so obviously in danger.

"Thank you. My father is old and I don't want to risk him becoming involved. He doesn't know that I work for MI6. He's rather old fashioned and wouldn't approve of my job. In the Arab culture, women stay home and bring up children. He is always asking when I'm going to get married and make him a grandfather. If you'd told me to get lost I would have gone abroad somewhere."

"That may still be the best option. I'll speak with my friend and see what I can find out. I offer no guarantees he will be able to help."

"I understand."

"Stay out of sight in here while I go update Afina and I'll organise some extra security for the bar."

"Thanks," Lara said.

Powell wasn't feeling very positive about the situation but tried to give an encouraging smile in response. If the American returned with some local police and an arrest warrant on some trumped up charge, they were going to be in big trouble. He couldn't get into a fight with genuine police officers.

CHAPTER SEVEN

Powell found Afina standing beside one of the tables. One of the customers at the table was using a credit card to pay their bill and Afina was putting it through the handheld machine. Powell caught her attention and used his eyes to signal he needed a word. A minute later the customers left and Afina walked over to Powell.

"You didn't tell me she was beautiful," Afina said without preamble.

"Who?" Powell replied innocently.

"You know who. Lara. She's beautiful."

"I guess she is quite attractive," Powell agreed. "But that's not important. Right now she's in big trouble and needs my help."

"Why you? She hardly knows you. You must have made a big impression on her when you were in Saudi Arabia."

"Lara knows I have a friend in MI5 and she needs his help. I think I was a last resort."

Powell hoped Afina's negative reaction to Lara was caused by her being protective of him and the bar rather than any misplaced jealousy. He'd said nothing to give her grounds to believe anything had occurred between him and Lara, when he was in Saudi. And seeing Lara again had confirmed any feelings he'd once had for her, were definitely confined to the past. There were too many conflicting memories.

Then again, why was he afraid to be honest with Afina about what happened in Saudi? He hadn't been unfaithful. He was an adult and he wasn't in a relationship with Afina at the time. In fact, he'd never been in that type of a relationship with Afina. He recognised where Afina was concerned, he was quite screwed up at times.

"I thought she worked for them already?" Afina questioned.

"Lara works for MI6," Powell explained patiently. "Or did until recently. They are the foreign security services. MI5 is the homeland security service. They are completely separate."

"Who were those men earlier?"

"I don't know yet but I'm going to see if Brian can help find out."

"Will they come back?"

"I hope not."

"Perhaps it would be better for all of us if Lara was to leave."

"Afina, she needs my help. I can't just send her away. And I don't believe you would do so either, knowing her life is in danger. But if you insist I will ask her to leave."

Afina said nothing for a moment. "You are too damned clever sometimes. You are not the sort of man to deny help to a woman in trouble. I was lucky enough to discover that for myself. Of course, she can stay. But you knew I would say that."

"Thank you." He had been certain of her response but it was still nice to be proved right. "Can I use the apartment to make a couple of calls?" He needed the privacy as he certainly didn't entirely trust Lara was telling him the whole story and he couldn't call from the bar.

"Of course. Say hello to Brian from me."

Powell went upstairs to the apartment, glad to escape Afina's bad mood and questions. He wasn't used to her being so grumpy. He hadn't been upstairs for a long time and it felt strange being back in what for him would always be Bella's apartment. There was no longer any photos of Bella on display, which Powell had packed away in a box and moved to his home when Afina decided to stay permanently in Brighton. Now there were photos of Afina's family everywhere and it made Powell seem an intruder in what had once been a second home.

The first call he made was to Jenkins, who had helped him get Angela Bennett's children out of Saudi Arabia. Powell was pleased to find him at home in South Wales and not working. Powell had only to say that he needed his help and Jenkins quickly agreed to set off for Brighton almost immediately. He asked no questions and Powell offered no explanations, simply saying he would explain everything when Jenkins arrived in Brighton.

The second call was to his friend Brian at MI5. Powell didn't want to say anything important over an open line so simply stated it was an emergency and he urgently needed a private conversation. Brian understood the emphasis on private and said he would call back in twenty minutes.

"Where are you?" Powell asked immediately, when Brian's name appeared as the caller.

"A coffee shop. What's up?"

"I've just had a visit from Lara."

"Lara? What does she want and why are you being paranoid about privacy?"

"Can you get down to Brighton tonight? I'll buy dinner."

"You can't tell me something more on the phone?"

"Better not."

"Are you in trouble?"

"Lara certainly is and by default I may be now as well."

"I can be at the bar about seven, if that's okay?"

"Perfect."

"I'm quite looking forward to meeting Lara, after everything you told me about her."

"We'll see you later… and Brian, don't tell anyone where you're going. I mean not anyone."

There was a brief pause before Brian said, "I won't." Then he added, "Make sure you have a good steak available tonight. I get the feeling I'm not going to enjoy what you have to tell me."

CHAPTER EIGHT

Baz was wondering why his contact Phoenix had changed the meeting place. Perhaps it was just because the operation was now underway and extra security was necessary. He was first to arrive at the small café, sat at a table outside and ordered tea. It was an old fashioned café not one of the modern style coffee shops from the west now flooding the cities. There were just a couple of locals sat at one other table.

He was looking forward to this meeting more than any other with Phoenix since he returned to his homeland almost two years ago. At their last meeting, Phoenix had provided the information about Fawwaz Al-Hashimi and informed Baz it was vital he passed it on to the English woman on a specific date. Baz was hoping Phoenix would have more important information for him today, which he could again trade for sex with Lara.

As Baz sipped his coffee, he wondered why he had been instructed to pass across information that would almost certainly lead to the capture of Al-Hashimi. Baz didn't know the man personally but the timing of when he gave Lara the name, so soon after the bombing of the London marathon was surely more than just a coincidence.

Why Phoenix had told him to betray such a hero was almost beyond comprehension but he understood there was a bigger plan at play and this was an important part of that plan. Baz had allowed Lara to think she had ensnared him for this very reason. He was able to feed her information and she no longer questioned its integrity.

Baz was beginning to get uncomfortable. He had drank two coffees and Phoenix was almost twenty minutes late. He had never previously been late for a meeting and Baz was worried there was a problem. He cast anxious glances around but there seemed no reason for concern. He was supposed to receive a coded message if Phoenix was unable to meet.

He was wondering how much longer he should wait, when his phone announced the arrival of a message and he expectantly picked it up to check.

The message was short and simple: *Sorry but I cannot make coffee today. My husband has come home unexpectedly.*

Baz was both annoyed and worried. He didn't like having been kept waiting so long before being told the meeting was cancelled. It showed a lack of respect. However, his overwhelming feeling was concern there was a problem. It was time to leave.

Baz again looked around but there was just the normal mixture of locals going about their everyday business. He called the waiter over and settled the bill. He left a large tip to save the man going inside for change. His car was parked about fifty metres along the road and he was developing a strong desire to be behind the wheel. He wanted to be well away from here, as soon as possible.

He had only walked a few paces when he glanced quickly behind. It was a sudden and unexpected move, which gave no time for anyone following to react. There was no sign of trouble. Nobody seemed to be paying him any interest. He relaxed a little and continued walking to his car.

He was frustrated on more than one level by the cancelled meeting. No information meant no leverage for enjoying more pleasure with Lara. He sighed at the thought of her body. He was indeed fortunate she was a beautiful woman. If she had been plain and unexciting, it would still have been necessary to sleep with her in order to become her spy within the organisation. Never before had his work been so pleasurable.

He opened his car door and climbed clumsily into the seat. He knew he could do with losing a few pounds but sex was the only form of exercise he enjoyed. The thought made him smile.

Next time he would have to insist on Lara allowing him more time to enjoy her body. She was a dish that should not be served cold and it took time to warm her up. She pretended not to enjoy sex with him but he knew the truth.

There was a man crossing the road in front of his car. Baz paid the man no attention and turned on the ignition. He was about to pull out when he realised the man had stopped in front of his car and turned towards him.

In what seemed like slow motion, Baz saw the man raise his arm and in his hand was a gun, which was pointing directly at him through the windscreen. Baz desperately tried to duck but he was far too slow to react. He was squeezed too tightly into his seat and he knew there was no escape.

The first bullet caught him in the throat and made him slump back in his seat. Baz's hand flew to his throat and tried to stem the flow of blood but it was an impossible task. The blood poured out over his hand and down his shirt.

He was certain Phoenix had betrayed him, just as he had betrayed Al-Hashimi. His brain was telling him he must get away but he was powerless to move. The car engine was running. If he could just reach the steering wheel.

Baz saw the man take careful aim for a second time and squeeze the trigger. The bullet entered his head through his nose and he was to all extents and purposes dead but the assassin walked to the side of the car, opened the driver's door and put two more bullets into Baz's head.

CHAPTER NINE

Brian and Jenkins arrived at the bar within ten minutes of each other and after getting them both a drink, Powell took them through to the office.

The surprise on Jenkins face when he spotted Lara was priceless. He glanced at Powell with a questioning look.

"I've heard much about you," Brian said, shaking Lara's hand. He was reluctant to let go. Powell had described her as attractive, which was a massive understatement.

"None of it good, I'm sure," Lara replied, smiling.

"Not true," Brian answered.

Powell was sure his friend was blushing like a schoolboy talking, for the first time, to the girl he secretly fancied. He suspected Lara often left men tongue tied or blushing.

Brian continued, "Powell always says he couldn't have brought the children home without your help. Angela Bennett is a personal friend of mine. In fact, it was me who introduced Angela to Powell so it's nice to be able to thank you in person at last, for what you did."

"I was glad to be able to help," Lara replied. "I took some convincing to help but Powell can be very persuasive."

Very diplomatically put, Powell thought.

"Good to see you again," Lara said, turning to Jenkins with outstretched hand.

Jenkins gave a perfunctory shake of her hand. "Good for us or good for you? I doubt it can be good for both of us."

"I'm sorry about the past, I was just doing my job. Believe it or not, I was pleased you managed to get the children back to their mother. Their father is a nasty piece of work."

Powell spoke up before Jenkins could respond further. "Anyone hungry? I've reserved a quiet table for us."

"I'm looking forward to your best steak," Brian answered.

"Famished," Jenkins admitted. "A large rare steak with all the trimmings sounds perfect."

"Is Afina joining us?" Brian asked.

"No, she and Mara are going to a concert tonight and I'm meant to be running the bar. It's the first night she's had off in a long while and to be honest, the less she knows about this, the better. I don't want to involve her in more danger."

"When I arrived, she didn't seem her normal bubbly self," Brian commented. "I think she's feeling excluded. Did you explain to her you're just worried for her safety?"

"Not really," Powell admitted.

"You two have been through a lot together, you need to speak to her."

"I'll update her in the morning," Powell promised. Perhaps a good night out would put her in a better mood. Although while Lara was around, he suspected her bad mood was likely to remain. "Let's go eat," he suggested. "If you all follow me, I'll show you to our table."

Once everyone was seated, Afina appeared at the table. "We're leaving now," Afina informed them. "If you're sure you can all manage without us?"

"We're fine thanks, Afina," Powell replied. Then he remembered what Brian had suggested. "If you're around in the morning, I'd like to speak to you."

"I'm always here in the morning."

"Good. Enjoy your evening."

"What concert are you seeing?" Jenkins asked.

"Jason Derulo."

"Brilliant. I'd love to see him."

"You know who he is?" Powell asked, obviously surprised.

"Of course I do. Don't you?"

"Never heard of him."

"But he was playing earlier," Jenkins pointed out.

"We play music all day in here. I can't know every singer."

"Dinosaurs don't appreciate good music," Afina said smiling.

"Don't you need to be leaving?" Powell hinted. "Can you please send Neill across and we'll order some drinks."

After Afina left, Lara asked, "Where is Afina from?"

"Romania," Powell answered.

"What was Brian referring to when he said you had both been through a lot?" Lara quizzed.

"That's personal," Powell replied succinctly, cutting off any further questions. He didn't feel he had the right to describe the hell Afina had been through. It was her story to tell. "Lara, I think it's time for you to replay everything that has happened to you recently."

Lara took twenty minutes to tell her story, answering a few questions from Brian along the way and stopping only for Neill to take and deliver their orders for drinks.

As the story neared its conclusion, Powell could see Brian become increasingly concerned.

"As you know, I'm Director of Training and I no longer have any day-to-day operational involvement," Brian explained. "I know all our resources have been focused on finding the marathon bomber but I've never heard of this Al-Hashimi. As far as I'm aware we're still searching for the bomber."

"Would you know if Al-Hashimi had been captured?" Powell asked.

"In normal circumstances I would know but if what Lara described has happened, then whoever has sanctioned it would want to keep the list of people in the know to an absolute minimum. There would be no reason for me to be included."

"I'm not lying," Lara emphasised.

"Sorry, I didn't mean to imply you are lying. What I do know for sure is that we still have everyone focused on finding this bomber. To knowingly waste our resources in that way would require a huge cover up. Frankly, I'm thinking this Al-Hashimi isn't the marathon bomber but a different terrorist. It's the only possible explanation. Even then I have to say, I'm doubtful we've even been informed about this Al-Hashimi."

"Is that really possible?" Powell probed.

"Lara passed her information to her superiors in MI6," Brian answered. "Perhaps they never passed the name to us, which would be highly irregular but might be explained by their intention to find him and operate off the grid."

"You mean extract information in ways that MI5 wouldn't condone?" Powell quizzed.

"This is all conjecture and highly unlikely," Brian stated. "There would be hell to pay once it was out in the open and it's not the sort of thing you could keep covered up for ever."

"Twenty five years ago, things were done in Ireland, which to this day have remained secret," Powell mentioned. "It is feasible."

Powell noticed the small, almost imperceptible movement of Brian's head as he set an empty glass back down on the table.

"I need to empty the tank before I start again," Brian announced, standing.

"Think I'll do the same," Powell agreed.

Once in the toilets, Powell checked the cubicles were empty. "What do you think?" he asked, once satisfied they were alone.

"I'm not sure but I don't like what I've heard. Do you think Lara is telling the truth?"

"Broadly I do but it's possible she isn't telling us everything."

"It seems likely those men who paid you a visit today will be back, whoever they work for."

"I agree, that's why Jenkins is here."

"It's not going to be easy for me to verify any of this," Brian said. "If I ask too many questions, I'm just likely to attract attention and bring a whole load of trouble down on all of us… There is another way."

"Which is?" Powell asked.

"Throw her to the wolves. You don't owe her anything."

"I can't do that."

Brian let out a sigh. "Thought you'd say that. I'll see what I can find out but in the meantime you need to be very careful."

They had just left the toilets when Powell's phone rang. He decided to take the call as it was Angela Bennett.

"Hi Angela."

"Powell, I've just been notified Baz is dead."

Powell was halfway back to the table. He immediately stopped and turned away from the table and Lara in particular. "Baz is dead? What happened?"

"I had an email from his new wife. She felt I should know because of the children. He was shot in his car."

"When did it happen?"

"Two days ago."

The timing coincided with the attempt on Lara's life and it seemed more than just a coincidence. "Are you okay?" Powell asked.

"I'm fine. I don't wish to appear callous but it's something of a relief. I can stop worrying what he might be planning to do to get the children back. I just thought you'd want to know."

"As you say, it might be for the best. Thanks for letting me know. Have you told Karim and Laila?"

"No. I'm not sure I will, at least not in the near future. They've been through enough and they don't ever expect to see him again, anyway."

"If you need my help with anything don't hesitate to give me a call," Powell stressed. "I'll speak to you soon."

With the call finished, Powell turned to Brian, who had remained standing nearby. "Did you get that? Baz was murdered two days ago."

"This is getting serious," Brian warned. "Let's see what Lara has to say for herself."

CHAPTER TEN

Phoenix had entered Britain without any problems. At passport control he felt like challenging why this small island had the audacity to call themselves 'Great' but of course he said nothing. He was happy to have arrived at the scene of what would be his most memorable victory. It had been a long journey to this point. From the early days spent fighting Russians to the current time, it felt like his whole life there had been an enemy to fight. For the first time in a long time, he felt they were on the brink of defeating the British and Americans.

The soft capitalists were experiencing doubt about continuing to wage war, faced with significant losses and an angry public fed up of soldiers coming home in body bags and refugees flooding their shores. This was the price they paid for meddling in the affairs of other countries.

Phoenix was pleased that the plan was progressing as expected. Baz was dead and he was the only man who knew that the information, which would inevitably be tortured out of Al-Hashimi, was in fact intentional misinformation. The authorities would be looking in the wrong direction when Phoenix's plan came to fruition. They would be expecting an attack but at the wrong time and the wrong venue. Such subterfuge had become necessary with security so tight at every large event, especially such an important conference.

Recent attacks in Europe had been very successful but they had all been targeted at the public. Phoenix had become fed up with the West targeting the leaders of ISIS with their bombs. It was time to strike back at their leaders and make them pay the price for their crimes. There was one figure in particular he held responsible above all others and this was their target.

The last contribution of Baz had been to secure the Saudi passport, which Phoenix had used to enter Britain. He knew he would sleep sounder knowing Baz was not alive to reveal the name under which he was travelling. He was a Saudi business man visiting the country to attend exhibitions and discuss potential partnerships with various companies. He had pre-booked his tickets for an exhibition at Olympia and his cover story was solid.

It hurt Phoenix that a man like Baz should meet such an easy end and a hero like Al-Hashimi, should have to experience waterboarding and spend the rest of his life in prison. Baz was a fool, although he had been a useful fool for quite some time. He had dared to believe he was important in the organisation but he was not a true believer. He was a weak man and weak men could not be trusted. He would always put his own interests before all others.

While Phoenix was sure Al-Hashimi would only give up his information when the torture became unbearable, he was equally sure Baz would squeal at the mere suggestion of pain. Perhaps it was the result of too much time spent living in England, which had weakened his spirit. He could not hide his desire for the Lara woman, who was the worst of creatures, a mongrel created with a mixture of Arabic and Western blood. In time, she would also pay the price for her scheming.

Phoenix took the underground train from Heathrow airport to London and then walked the short distance to Bayswater. He was the first to arrive but soon he was to be joined by two comrades and together they would wreak vengeance against the enemy.

The American met his contact at a private and very exclusive club in Mayfair. It was definitely a cut above the normal places he met his employers and when he gave the name of Brown, he was expected and shown to a small meeting room. It wasn't his real name but one he had used for a number of years since becoming a private contractor.

The CIA had suggested they were no longer a good fit for his specific skills. There was too much oversight of their activities and being no longer employed made plausible deniability of his actions so much easier. That they intended to continue using him was not in doubt. With the war they were fighting against terror, his skills were considered a necessary evil. They could not be fully effective if they had to fight with their hands tied behind their backs. The terrorists had no inhibitions about how they fought the war. And he was good at what he did. He always extracted every last piece of information from his captives.

Brown enjoyed his work. He hated terrorists with a passion and had no sympathy for anyone who sought to kill innocent civilians. In his view, a war should be fought on the battlefield not in a shopping mall or cinema.

But the terrorists had made their bed and now they had to lie in it or more precisely, they had to sit in his chair and tell him everything they knew. It was his job to prevent future atrocities by getting information from prisoners about their contacts and operations. There was nothing more satisfying than extracting a piece of information that led to subsequent arrests.

The door to the room opened and the Englishman entered. Brown didn't particularly like him but he paid well.

"Why is the Saliba woman still alive?" the Englishman asked without ceremony.

"I wanted to check with you what would be acceptable collateral damage."

"It is vital she is removed immediately, which I believe are exactly the same words I used at our previous meeting. What is it you didn't understand about my instructions?"

"She's in Brighton, staying with someone who owns a bar. I didn't know if civilian casualties were acceptable."

"Within reasonable limits and if you deem it absolutely necessary."

"Sorry but our idea of reasonable limits may be very different. I know you British are rather squeamish about things. Please be more precise." Brown didn't want any comeback at a later date.

"Reasonable is whatever it takes to silence her. The damn woman has already tried to raise the alarm about what she saw. Fortunately, we can still keep a lid on her but time is running out. We don't want to draw unnecessary attention to ourselves so an accident would be preferable but do whatever is required. Are you clear this time about what I want?"

"Crystal," Brown answered. He didn't like the way the Englishman talked down to him but he was paying the bills and calling the shots. He was an upper class shit who had probably never got his hands dirty in his life. There was always someone else to do his dirty work.

"Good. The longer this woman is at large, the greater the risk to our plans."

"I'll take action immediately," Brown promised.

"Please do so or we may need to find someone who better understands my instructions."

Brown didn't appreciate threats but he bit his tongue. He would have liked to tell him where to stick his job but that wasn't a good idea. The money was good and the Englishman might have use of him again in the future. He also probably had a load of contacts and personal recommendation was how Brown got most of his business. He didn't understand all the details surrounding his current job but it was definitely a high profile operation and he didn't want negative feedback flowing back to the States.

The Englishman turned and left the room without saying anything further. Brown was pleased he'd been given almost carte blanche. He hadn't liked the way Powell prevented him taking the woman in the bar. He hoped Powell might try to stop him a second time. There would be a different result next time.

CHAPTER ELEVEN

Brian had given a great deal of thought as to what to do next. The previous evening in Brighton, he had listened to Lara's story and been left in no doubt she was telling the truth. There really was no reason for her to invent what she had seen and Powell had testified to the threat posed by the three men who visited the bar. The death of Baz just seemed to confirm the wheels of some type of plot were in motion but who was involved was impossible to assess.

Brian had asked for a meeting with his boss, the Assistant Director General. The ADG was responsible for all the non-operational side of MI5. That meant areas like Finance, IT and Training. His equivalent on the operations side was the Deputy Director General, who ran the likes of counter-terrorism and counter-espionage. It was the DDG who would have the answers to Brian's questions but he needed to go through the right channels. The ADG was a long-time colleague and friend, who Brian trusted.

Brian was apprehensive as he took the chair opposite the ADG, despite having sat there many times before. He enjoyed his work and didn't want to put his job at risk by putting his nose where it wasn't welcome but felt he had few other options. He looked around the office while the ADG finished reading something on his desk. It was a large elegant room that wouldn't look out of place as the study in a country mansion. If it was meant to be intimidating and convey the importance of the occupant, it certainly succeeded.

"Hello, Brian. What can I do for you?" the ADG asked pleasantly, looking up from his papers. "Barbara said it was urgent but I'm afraid I don't have much time."

"Would you please humour me and allow me to ask if you know the name Fawwaz Al-Hashimi?" After telling Lara of Baz's death, she had volunteered the name of the terrorist, irrelevant of the Official Secrets Act. Baz's death had removed the last vestige of doubt in any of their minds. Someone wanted Lara dead.

"It's not a name I know. Now what's this all about?"

Brian had studied closely the ADG's face as he threw out the name but could detect no hint of recognition or surprise in the ADG's reaction to hearing the name. "One further question if you don't mind. Do you believe the marathon bomber is still at large?"

"What nonsense is this, Brian?" The ADG asked, having lost his good humour and sounding quite irritated. "You know as well as I do that we are still hunting the bomber."

"That was my understanding before last night…" Brian wavered, there was still time to back off.

"I think you'd better tell me what happened last night."

"You know I have a friend, Powell…"

"He was the one recovered the Bennett children?"

"Yes that's him. Worked for us twenty years ago. Well, while he was in Saudi he met a woman called Lara Saliba. She was born in the UK to a Lebanese father and an English mother. She works for MI6 based in Saudi Arabia. I spoke with her and Powell last night in Brighton. She has an interesting story to tell…"

"Well get on it with it man. I haven't got all day."

Brian was at the point of no return. "She has or I should say had a contact in Saudi called Abdul Rashid, who was the ex-husband of Angela Bennett. He was murdered two days ago. About the same time an attempt was made on Lara's life."

"This is all very interesting but what the hell does it have to do with us?"

"A short time back, Rashid passed Lara the name Fawwaz Al-Hashimi as a terrorist bomber, who had recently entered the UK. In fact he'd entered just before the marathon bombing took place."

"Is this Abdul Rashid reliable?"

"I understand he had proven himself very reliable. Anyway, Lara passed the information up the line. A couple of days ago Lara was summoned to Vauxhall to help with the interrogation of Fawwaz Al-Hashimi. She was taken by helicopter to some place in the country where she observed Al-Hashimi being tortured in ways that can only be described as medieval…"

"One minute," the ADG interrupted. He picked up his desk phone and said, "Barbara, push all my meetings back thirty minutes and see if you can get me a meeting with both the DDG and the DG sometime today. If only one is possible then go for that and as soon as possible." He replaced the receiver and turned back to Brian. "You tell an interesting story. Go on."

"Yesterday, three men including the man Lara had seen torture Al-Hashimi, went to Powell's bar and tried to force Lara to go with them. She refused and Powell forced them to leave…"

"How did he do that?"

"Powell can be very persuasive. But he's outgunned at three to one and the odds could be a lot worse. Who knows what resources these men can call upon. I'm sure they won't just give up and Powell is a very good friend of mine. I don't care too much about Lara but I don't want to see Powell get hurt. He's an obstinate sod and is likely to go to any lengths to protect Lara. So I'm here to find out what the hell is going on."

"The short answer is I have no idea. It may be there is a bigger picture and I'm simply not in the loop but that is highly unlikely."

"The bigger picture shouldn't include medieval torture. Last I heard that was illegal."

"We aren't like the Americans, even waterboarding is off limits."

"Which raises another interesting point. The man doing the torturing was American."

The phone on the ADG's desk buzzed. He picked it up and listened for a few seconds. "Thanks, Barbara," he said and replaced the receiver. "I have a meeting with the DG in an hour. Start again at the beginning and tell me everything."

CHAPTER TWELVE

Brown didn't like having multiple bosses demanding his time. There were only so many hours in a day. Although the Englishman wanted him to move immediately against the woman, he first had to satisfy his American boss. All being well, both of them would be happy by the end of what was going to be a long evening.

Brown didn't know London very well but his instructions had been specific and it wasn't difficult to find Old Compton Street. He took the tube to Leicester Square and then had a five minute walk to the pub. The streets were busy with people out for a good time. Many of them had just finished work and were getting a drink or two before heading back home.

As he approached the entrance, he wasn't surprised to find a bouncer on the door. There were a few people hanging around outside smoking. He received several appreciative stares from some of the men, who were all dressed far more casually than his suit. He'd stuffed his tie inside his jacket pocket and undone the top two buttons on his shirt to try and appear more casual. Hopefully he looked like someone who had just finished work.

"Hello," Brown said in a thick American accent as he approached the bouncer. "This is a gay bar, isn't it? Only someone at the office recommended it to me."

"It definitely is," one of the smokers answered. "Best gay pub in London."

Brown turned towards the smoker. "I hear there's usually a good show."

"That will be much later in the evening," the smoker explained.

"No problem. I want to try some of your warm British beer. We don't get warm beer back home."

"Good luck," the smoker replied. "Personally I prefer the cold lager."

"I see your laws are the same as ours in the States. Can't bloody smoke anywhere."

"Afraid not."

Brown turned back towards the pub entrance.

"Can I take a look inside your briefcase?" the bouncer requested.

"Of course. I came straight from work so stuck with the suit and the case." Brown opened it, revealing a few harmless papers.

The bouncer gave it only a perfunctory look inside before saying, "Have a good evening."

"I might see you inside," the smoker said, smiling.

"Hope so," Brown replied with a smile as he went inside.

He was surprised by how relatively small the pub was. There were tables around the side, which all seemed occupied and a stage at one end. He wanted to get a seat if possible.

"Hi again," the smoker said, returning inside. "You look a bit lost. I'm Danny. I'm here with my friend Jim. Do you want to join us?"

"Thanks. That would be great as I don't really know anyone in London. I'm just here for work for a few days."

Danny led the way to one of the tables where his friend, who Brown assumed didn't smoke, was sitting. After introductions, Brown offered to get the drinks in and went to the bar to buy beers.

Returning to the table, Brown looked at his new friends. He guessed they were both in their late twenties, which made them four or five years younger. They were skinny and dressed in similar jeans and t-shirts.

"Are you guys a couple?" Brown asked.

"We are but we still like to party," Jim answered.

"Partying sounds good to me," Brown smiled. "Cheers," he said, raising his pint.

"Do you work out?" Danny asked. "You look very fit."

"I like to keep in shape. I go to the gym most days," Brown admitted. "What about you guys?"

"We're more into going out to the pub," Danny laughed.

"Glad you do otherwise I wouldn't have met you."

Brown drank his pint of bitter slowly in comparison to the others, who were soon both ready for a refill.

"You enjoying that?" Danny asked. "Only you're drinking it real slow."

"I think I might have a cold beer next. This is lukewarm and tastes more like piss than beer. You Brits have some funny habits."

"I'll get you a pint of San Miguel," Danny offered and went to the bar.

Three pints later and Brown decided it was time for him to complete his business. He waited for Danny to come back from having a smoke. He reached under the table and opened his briefcase. He slipped his hand under the false bottom and pressed the timer.

"I need to make a phone call to free up the rest of my evening," Brown announced. "That's if you guys are still up for some more partying?"

"Absolutely," Danny confirmed.

"Get the beers in, Jim and I'll be back in a minute."

Brown walked outside the pub with his phone held against his ear to dissuade anyone from trying to engage him in conversation. He headed past the smokers and kept walking. He was almost back at the tube station when he heard the explosion. Danny and Jim's evening had definitely ended with a bang!

CHAPTER THIRTEEN

Brian decided it was best to pay another visit to Brighton. He needed to relay the DG's findings to Powell and Lara.

Brian found Powell sitting alone at a table in the bar, drinking a whisky and studying menus. There was already a spare glass alongside a half empty bottle on the table.

"Want one?" Powell asked, indicating his whisky. He was bored of studying the proposed new menus and happy for some company. He was though pleased that Afina had at least consulted him about the menu changes.

"A large one, please. It's been that kind of day."

Powell poured a large measure and handed the glass to Brian. "So tell me about it."

"Where's Lara?"

"Upstairs in Afina's apartment," Powell replied. "Do you want me to get her?"

"No. Let's go to your office and I can update you first." Brian could see that Afina was busy behind the bar so they would have the office to themselves.

"As bad as that?" Powell joked.

Brian didn't reply but he picked up the whisky bottle and walked towards the office. Powell picked up his drink and followed. He closed the door behind them, took his usual seat behind the desk and waited expectantly for Brian's news.

Brian broke the silence. "I decided it was too important to mess about trying to gather bits of info from old friends so I met with my boss who is the ADG," Brian explained. "I've known him almost as long as I've known you and I trust him. He was shocked by what I told him and went to see the DG. Then in the afternoon the three of us met."

"It's funny to think how when we were new recruits we lived in awe of the DG," Powell remarked.

"He's a decent guy," Brian replied. "So firstly I have to tell you that neither of them has ever heard the name Al-Hashimi. They are still hunting for the marathon bomber and you can imagine their shock was fairly high on the Richter scale, when I told them MI6 definitely knew him and indeed had him stashed away somewhere. The ADG told me the DG almost had a coronary on the spot when he first heard my story."

"Do you believe them both?" Powell asked.

"I believe they knew nothing about Al-Hashimi but I'm not sure I entirely believe what they are now telling me… The DG says he spoke with his equivalent in MI6 and they also have no knowledge of an Al-Hashimi, and they too are still hunting the marathon bomber."

"That doesn't sound right," Powell said.

"I agree and it may be that they have discovered a mess and decided to sweep the truth under the carpet."

"That's the only possible explanation because Lara didn't decide off her own back to come to England to interrogate Al-Hashimi. Someone with some pretty big clout in MI6 has stashed Al-Hashimi away, hired helicopters and everything else. Unless we're missing something?"

Brian topped up both their whiskies. "You're missing the most important point," Brian said, having tasted his whisky. "If the head of MI6 says they have never heard of Al-Hashimi, then where in the chain of command has the information from Baz via Lara disappeared? I think we can believe she passed it to her boss in Saudi."

"The same boss, who the moment Lara mentions she didn't like what she saw happen to Al-Hashimi, tells her to say nothing and he will look into it, except she suddenly finds her life threatened."

"That's the man," Brian agreed.

"So Baz, who passed Lara the information is now dead and Lara probably should be. Someone has tried to silence the two people who knew Al-Hashimi is in the UK."

"Perhaps someone inside ISIS discovered Baz had passed the information to Lara and was simply trying to protect Al-Hashimi so he could carry out his attacks."

"The timing doesn't really work. Al-Hashimi was already a prisoner by the time of the attempt on Lara's life," Powell answered doubtfully.

"Then killing Lara was just them getting rid of the person they blame for recruiting Baz."

"Possibly," Powell agreed. "But why hasn't Lara's boss passed on the information about Al-Hashimi to his superiors in MI6?"

"We don't know for sure he hasn't. He's passed the information to someone as otherwise Al-Hashimi wouldn't have been captured and tortured."

"And the man doing the torturing was American. Could the CIA be somehow involved?"

"Doesn't seem very likely."

"Irish terrorism was so much easier to deal with. I honestly don't know how you cope with today's world."

"I'm not sure we do cope," Brian admitted. "We're a bit like Canute trying to push back the tide."

"I don't suppose the DG had any suggestions for what we do next?" Powell asked without much hope.

"Keep your heads down for a couple of days while the big boys check out what's going on. Perhaps a holiday for you and Lara would be a good idea?"

"Very funny! You want to see Afina put one of our kitchen knives in my back?"

"I thought your relationship with Afina was purely platonic."

"It is but… it's not as simple as that."

"You two need to sort out your feelings before someone gets hurt."

"And a knife in the back would definitely hurt so I don't think going away with Lara is a good idea."

"So what will you do?"

"Stay alert and try to keep out of trouble."

"Okay, I'll let you know what develops at the office. The DG has promised to keep me regularly updated but I take that with a pinch of salt. He'll speak to me when he needs something. Right now I suspect he's more concerned about covering his back with the politicians."

"I thought you said you liked him?"

"He's perfectly pleasant but you don't get to be DG without knowing how to ingratiate yourself with politicians. They are his masters."

"I guess so," Powell agreed.

"Let's get Lara down here and tell her what we know," Brian suggested.

"It's more like what we don't know," Powell said, finishing his glass. "I'll go get her."

A breathless Powell and Afina came back into the office ten minutes later.

"You took your time," Brian remarked. "What have you two been up to?"

His voice carried a sexual innuendo.

"We were watching the news," Powell responded. "There's been another bomb. A gay pub in the centre of London about half an hour ago. There may be as many as twenty dead."

Brian sat upright. "Well that wasn't Al-Hashimi's work. Was it a suicide bomber?"

"Too early to tell. There's been a message though sent to a national newspaper claiming it was the work of ISIS. Gays were targeted as being an abomination and a crime against God."

"Sounds like their kind of twisted thinking. I better skip dinner and head back to town. It's going to be all hands to the pump. You can update Lara on the day's events."

CHAPTER FOURTEEN

Powell received a parking permit as the owner of the bar and always parked his BMW just a minute's walk away. As he left the bar with Lara and Jenkins, he studied the vicinity to see if he could spot any sign of imminent danger, though he wasn't sure exactly what he expected to see. Danger could come in many guises but there were at least no men in dark suits and shades hanging around on the street corner.

He had watched Lara get quite tipsy as the evening wore on. Brian's update from his meetings with the DG and in particular, the news that Al-Hashimi was an unknown name within both MI5 and MI6, had come as a huge shock. Added to the previous night's news about the death of Baz, Powell could see that Lara was struggling to cope with the fact her world, as she thought she knew it, was falling apart. There was no explanation for what had happened but for certain she felt extremely vulnerable and in danger. The easy access to alcohol meant she had started drinking early evening and although she had not gone mad, by the end of the evening she was definitely feeling the effects.

They reached the car without incident and Jenkins held the door open so Lara could sit in the back, before joining Powell in the front. Powell pulled away and he could see in his rear view mirror, first Lara's eyes closing, followed by her disappearing from view as she fell sideways on the back seat.

As they drove the five minute journey to his house, Powell was lost in thought. He had spent the latter part of the evening reflecting on the bomb in London. It reminded him of his days in MI5, when fighting Irish terrorism occupied his every waking moment. It had been a time when people in London and other cities were very aware of the danger of bombs, which became a regular occurrence. The big difference was that the IRA didn't have suicide bombers, which reduced the threat when compared to the current times.

Powell wondered if Al-Hashimi was just a small part of a new campaign of coordinated attacks. Perhaps there were multiple cells operating, intent on destroying lives and property. It was a sobering thought and had stopped Powell from having too many drinks.

When they arrived at the house, Jenkins put his arm around Lara as she staggered getting out of the car. Powell led the way and opened the front door. He looked behind and could see Jenkins was struggling trying to support Lara and get her up the steps.

As a result, Powell didn't reach immediately for the light switch but stepped back and took Lara under one arm so the two of them could carry her up the steps. As he came back to the front door and reached for the light switch he halted a second away from lighting his hallway.

"Do you smell something?" Powell asked.

Jenkins took in a deep breath through his nose. "That's gas."

"Let's put her back in the car."

They half carried, half dragged Lara back to the car and pushed her onto the back seat where she lay down muttering something about being tired.

"You stay here," Powell said. "I'll check on the house."

"Be careful. It only takes a spark," Jenkins warned.

Powell retraced his steps to the front door. He made no attempt to turn on the light. Basic training at MI5 included awareness of how to manipulate a light socket to cause the spark needed to create a gas explosion.

The smell of gas was slightly less by the open front door but as he took a couple of steps into the house, the smell returned. He took a deep breath of fresh air and walked quickly to the kitchen. He opened the windows and then turned off the cooker. The door of the cooker was wide open and he knew with certainty, he hadn't left it that way.

He moved through the other downstairs rooms, opening all the windows as he went until he was satisfied he'd done everything possible to air the rooms. There was still a strong presence of gas but it was easing. He returned to join Jenkins.

"Someone's paid us a visit," Powell confirmed. "Give it a bit of time and then I'll check for how they may have intended to ignite the gas. I suspect I'll find a dodgy hallway light."

"This is pretty serious," Jenkins stated.

"That's probably an understatement. I'll give Brian a call and let him know about our visitors. He needs to find out what the hell is going on."

Powell took his phone from his pocket and as he pushed the call button, a shadow moved across his periphery vision. A few houses down on the other side of the road, someone had darted out from behind a car and crossed the road. Powell turned in the direction of what he was sure was danger but couldn't see anyone and for a second wondered if his imagination was working overtime.

"Did you see something?" Jenkins asked.

"I thought I did."

"We're terribly exposed standing around out here. We should get Lara in the house."

Powell was in two minds what to do but his mind was made up for him by the sight of a man briefly sticking his head out from behind the car, where Powell suspected he had been hiding since crossing the road. He was obviously checking what they were planning to do. Trying to drag Lara out of the car while she was asleep and get her in the house safely didn't appeal.

"Get in the car," Powell ordered.

Jenkins ran around to the passenger side and Powell quickly climbed in the driver's side. A glance in the rear view mirror as he pulled away, revealed the man hiding behind the car now standing, looking in their direction. The front door was still open but Powell thought that the least of his problems as he accelerated. He had noticed the car pulling out from across the road, before stopping for a second to allow the man on the pavement to jump inside.

"We have company," Powell announced.

Jenkins twisted in his seat to look at the car behind. "They'll be armed."

"I have a weapon at the bar, in my office safe."

"Not sure we're going to make it that far."

"Call Afina," Powell said. "Ask her to have the front door open for us. I don't want to be fumbling with a key."

Jenkins did as asked and explained to Afina they were being followed.

"How many of them are there?" Powell asked after Jenkins finished.

Jenkins again looked out the back window. "Three I think."

Despite it being after midnight there was still a fair amount of traffic. Powell thought it might be sufficient witnesses to prevent the car behind from trying to ram them or do anything too radical. He drove fast and was pleased the late hour meant it would be possible to park right outside the bar.

He had to slow as the cars ahead stopped for a traffic light that was turning red. He cast a nervous glance in his mirror to confirm the car was still directly behind. He didn't like the idea of coming to a stop and being trapped between cars.

At the last moment, Powell accelerated and pulled out onto the wrong side of the road to overtake the cars in front. Up ahead, he could see a car starting to turn the corner, heading in his direction. Powell swung his car back in front of the queuing cars just in time and turned left. He'd seen the look of horror on the face of the other driver as the crash was narrowly averted.

Powell again checked in his rear mirror and was pleased to see the other car hadn't been foolish enough to follow. It would give them a much needed minute's head start. The men following would know where they were headed and for a second Powell thought about changing direction but he needed answers and the starting point was the American, who was almost certainly one of the men in the following car.

CHAPTER FIFTEEN

Powell skidded to a stop directly in front of the bar, not remotely concerned about parking restrictions. There was still no sign of the following car. He and Jenkins were both out of the car quickly. Jenkins opened the rear door, leaned in and tried to scoop Lara up in his arms. She responded by immediately lashing out with her feet and caught him in the thigh.

"It's me, Jenkins," he shouted, taking a step backwards to avoid her flailing feet. He was concerned she had only just missed kicking him in the balls. "We need to get you out of here."

Lara was slow to react, obviously still suffering from a mixture of tiredness and alcohol.

"For God's sake, Lara. Get out the fucking car," Jenkins urged.

"Okay, I'm coming," she replied but still barely moved.

Jenkins was joined on the pavement by Powell.

Seeing Lara's lack of progress, Powell shouted, "Can you please hurry up, Lara. We're in danger."

"Fuck," Jenkins swore, looking down the street and spotting the car.

Lara was by now half out the car and placed her feet on the pavement. She tried to stand but fell back into the car. She sat giggling for a second. Jenkins reached towards her and grabbed her by one arm, forcefully helping her to stand.

"Jenkins, I'll ask you for your help if I need it," Lara said, shaking her arm free of his grip.

"Lara, your American friend is in that car," Powell said pointing. "We need to get in the bar right now." Even as Powell said it he felt a sense of impending doom. The car had stopped just a short distance further down the road and the men were already heading in their direction.

Lara looked towards where Powell was pointing but didn't seem to understand the significance of the car.

"Get her inside," Powell said, as he turned to face the three oncoming men.

Jenkins had Lara around the waist and lifted her in a fireman's lift over his shoulder before she knew what was happening and rushed for the bar entrance, despite her protests.

The three men started running towards Powell and he took up a fighting stance, praying they wouldn't want to simply shoot him where he stood. As they outnumbered him, they were over confident.

The familiar American was in front of the others and came in swinging. Powell turned his back on him, stepped inside the flailing arm, grabbed it and used the man's momentum to throw him forwards to the ground.

Powell turned to face the other men and in the same movement he was lashing out with his leg, smashing it into the side of the head of one man, sending him crashing to the ground.

The last man immediately took a step back, realising he wasn't going to win a hand to hand fight and withdrew a gun from inside his jacket.

Powell was uncertain whether the man would fire. He stayed still, offering no threat.

"Shoot him," the American shouted from the floor.

Powell threw himself towards the man with the gun but he knew bullets were faster than even his honed reflexes. He heard the sound of the gun and then he barged the man to the floor. There had been no impact of a bullet. Thank God the man had been a poor shot.

As he lay on top of the man ready to grapple for the gun, Powell realised he was meeting no resistance. Powell briefly felt warm sticky blood on his hand but it wasn't his own.

He jumped to his feet expecting a renewed assault from the other two men. He turned to see neither man was moving and both were looking in the direction of the bar entrance where Afina was standing, pointing a gun at the two men.

"I'll take that," Jenkins said, emerging from the bar and taking hold of the gun. He had obviously deposited Lara somewhere inside.

Afina seemed frozen to the spot. She was staring at the man on the ground, who she had just shot. The moaning sounds suggested he was in great pain but also revealed he wasn't dead. He was clutching at his stomach and rolling from side to side.

Powell recognised the gun as the one he kept in the safe. He walked towards Afina and put a comforting arm around her shoulder. "You had no choice," he said. "You saved my life."

She looked at him and managed a half smile. He gripped her tighter and then turned to the man he had kicked in the head, who was crouched on the ground. "Pick up your colleague, put him in your car and get out of here."

The man didn't move but looked across at the American. "Jenkins, if he hasn't picked up that body within ten seconds, shoot him," Powell commanded.

"Be my pleasure," Jenkins said, aiming the gun at the man.

The man hurried to his feet and leaning down, picked up the injured man under one arm and supported him as they stumbled to the car. It took him a few minutes to manhandle the wounded man into the car and drive away. No one moved until the car was out of sight.

"You, inside," Powell commanded the American. "If he does anything out of place, Jenkins, you have my permission to put a bullet in him. Preferably somewhere it will really hurt but isn't fatal because he's beginning to piss me off."

Afina and Powell hung back while Jenkins followed the American into the bar. Powell waited a moment to make sure the car with the other two men had not decided to return, then guided Afina into the bar.

Lara was waiting inside for them. She seemed to have sobered up at the sight of the American and stood with her eyes fixed on him.

"Lara, please take Afina and go upstairs. Afina, you need to have a shower and wash thoroughly. You need to remove any evidence of having fired the gun. If you are ever forced to answer questions about who shot that man, you simply don't know. Neither of you were ever down here and have no knowledge of anything that has happened tonight."

"Wait a minute…" Afina started to argue.

"It's best," Lara cut her off. "Come on."

Afina reluctantly went with Lara.

"Take your jacket off," Powell instructed the American. "Drop it on the floor."

The American did as asked. The absence of a jacket revealed the American had a gun in a shoulder holster.

"Using two fingers gently take the weapon out and place it on the table. My friend Jenkins has something of a nervous disposition so I strongly advise you to move very slowly as otherwise it will be the last thing you ever do."

The American looked at Jenkins, who smiled, then he very slowly removed the gun and placed it on the table.

"Well done," Powell said. "Now move away from the table."

Powell picked up the gun and was reassured by its feel. An extra weapon certainly wouldn't go amiss.

We'll go to the office," Powell said and led the way.

CHAPTER SIXTEEN

Once inside the office, Powell motioned with his weapon towards one of the chairs. "Sit down," he said, pushing the American on the shoulder, when he was slow to sit.

Powell sat on the other side of the desk and played back the CCTV from outside the bar. The shooting had been captured clearly. He removed the tape and replaced it with an old tape from a few weeks earlier. He placed the recorded tape in his pocket. He was going to need to hide it somewhere safe once he'd dealt with the matter in hand. He didn't want to erase the tape because it could be useful in the unlikely event they ever needed to defend themselves in a court of law. On the other hand, it showed Afina as the person pulling the trigger and it would have to be a last resort before it was ever shared with anyone else.

Powell half expected the police to arrive at any moment. Though he hadn't seen anyone around when the man was shot, there was every possibility someone had seen what happened and dialled the emergency services. Certainly people would have heard the shot. The American's friends might even decide to return or call the police.

"Let's swap weapons," Powell said to Jenkins. After doing so, Powell then gripped his own gun tightly to register his fingerprints. If the police did arrive, he would claim responsibility for shooting the man.

Then he turned to the American. "You have a name?" Powell asked.

The American sat silently, staring straight ahead.

"Guess I'll just call you Yank in that case. So Yank, I want you to understand where I'm coming from. I don't particularly give a damn about how you treated Al-Hashimi. He probably deserved everything you did to him. Neither am I too bothered about why the heads of MI5 and MI6 have still never heard the name Al-Hashimi. What I do care about is my bar and my house. You tried to destroy my home and me with it earlier tonight so I want to know why? Why are you, someone I've never met before in my life, intent on killing me."

Again the American said nothing.

"Listen, I don't have your specialist skills for extracting information. I don't know how to prolong pain while keeping someone alive. I also doubt we have much time together so I'm going to keep this simple." He walked over to Jenkins and whispered in his ear.

Jenkins left the room but returned in less than a minute carrying a cushion from the bar. He handed it to Powell.

The American's eyes hadn't shifted despite the comings and goings. Powell wasn't certain he was going to get the answers he wanted.

"I don't suppose you want to volunteer what I need to know?" Powell asked pleasantly. Gaining no response, he continued, "Look, you aren't very old, younger than me for sure. If you don't tell me who you are working for, you are going to have to find a new line of work. There's not much demand for someone like you, if you're crippled."

Powell moved quickly and without further warning, holding the cushion directly in front of the gun, he fired. The noise of the shot was muffled by the cushion.

"Fucking hell!" the American screamed and grabbed for his leg.

"That's your final warning, Yank. I just winged your thigh. The next bullet will go through your kneecap. And the one after that through your other knee before I then work on your ankles… I don't have a lot of time." Powell raised the gun again as if to shoot. "I ask again. Why are you trying to kill me?"

"Wait! It's not you we were after. I was told to get rid of the woman and try to make it look like an accident. You were just in the wrong place."

"Well that makes me feel so much better," Powell replied sarcastically. "What's your name?"

"Brown."

"Who do you work for?"

The American hesitated and Powell took deliberate aim at his knee.

"Okay. Okay. I don't actually know much about him. My former boss at the Agency asked if I wanted some work…"

"So you worked for the CIA?" Powell interrupted.

"Until a couple of years ago."

"Continue."

"My boss put me in contact with a Mr Barnes."

"So you're a private contractor?"

"Yes but most of my work comes from old contacts."

"And what did Barnes want you to do?"

"Interrogate someone."

"Al-Hashimi?"

"Yes."

"So you discovered the information Barnes wanted?"

"Yes. He was pleased and I thought that was the end of the job but then he contacted me again and wanted me to get rid of the girl. I assumed he was tidying up loose ends."

"So who do you think Barnes works for?"

"I didn't really care but I assumed it was one of your government agencies. Probably MI5."

"If he did, don't you think he would have passed on the information about Al-Hashimi and he wouldn't be asking you to murder a member of MI6, which is where the girl in question works?"

"I gave up questioning instructions a long time ago. And in my experience, inter agency squabbles are two a penny."

"Did Al-Hashimi mention an attack tonight on the pub?"

"Not while I was questioning him but he may have done after I left."

"What planned attack did he mention?"

"The Tory party conference was to be his next target. The girl must have told you that."

Lara had indeed told Powell and he was just testing Brown. "Can you explain why the head of both MI5 and MI6 are completely unaware of such a planned attack?"

The American was thoughtful for a second. "Look, I regularly get used to extract information from terrorists using methods not palatable to governments. I actually believe what I do benefits everyone. If Barnes hasn't passed on the information then there must be a different agenda in play."

"Any idea what that might be?"

"My best guess would be someone must have a reason to want the attack to go ahead as planned."

"Then why bother to get the information in the first place?"

The American shrugged. "No idea. I've found it easier just to do as I'm told and not ask too many questions."

"Do you think Barnes is his real name?"

"Your guess is as good as mine."

"What happened to Al-Hashimi once you finished with him?"

"He was a broken man and giving up everything he knew so I wasn't needed any more but the questioning would have continued for days, maybe weeks or months. They would go over every detail of his life."

"Where is he being held?"

"I'm not sure. I was taken there by helicopter from London. It was somewhere in the country. He may even have been moved by now."

"So tell me more about Barnes. How did he contact you?"

"He called me and arranged to meet. I knew he'd been passed my contact details and I was expecting his call."

"Where did you meet?" Powell asked, hopeful of finally getting a worthwhile answer.

"The Mayfair Club. I would arrive, give my name and be shown to a meeting room. Barnes then came in and briefed me."

"Do you have a contact number for him?"

"I have an email address for emergencies but I haven't had to use it."

Powell pushed a piece of paper and pen in front of Brown. "Write the email down for me."

Powell picked the paper back up and studied the email address – johnemerichdalbergacton@gmail.com.

"Seems Barnes has a sense of humour," Powell commented, handing the paper to Jenkins.

Jenkins stared blankly at the paper. "Who the hell is that?"

"I think he's the man who said: Power corrupts: absolute power corrupts absolutely," Powell answered.

"He is," Brown agreed. "I googled the name."

"An email isn't much use for finding him," Powell admitted. "Describe Barnes to me," he demanded.

"Tall, average build, grey hair, about fifty. I'm not great on your accents but he speaks like he's important. A bit like your Queen."

"Any distinguishing marks?"

"No, you wouldn't notice him until he speaks. He's an arrogant prick… What are you going to do with me?"

"A good question…"

CHAPTER SEVENTEEN

Powell had secured the American in the basement. He was locked in the same place where a few months earlier, he had kept Victor prisoner. When he'd invested in the secure cage for protecting his valuable wines, he hadn't envisaged it doubling so regularly as a temporary cell.

Powell crept upstairs to see if Afina and Lara were asleep. He'd phoned Brian and MI5 were sending a car to collect the American, which would arrive in about an hour so going to bed wasn't an option. Powell could hear the girls talking as he neared the top of the stairs.

Powell was deeply concerned for Afina. She had proved herself able to handle extraordinarily difficult situations in the past but shooting someone could haunt the toughest of people. He certainly remembered the first person he shot and killed but at the actual time, he didn't have the chance to dwell on it as he was caught up in a gun battle with several members of the IRA.

It was later that evening he thought about the significance of having taken someone's life. He knew in truth he had little choice. It was kill or be killed. But despite the logic, Powell still felt troubled by what he'd done. The man he shot was only nineteen years old and looked like he'd barely started shaving. He was still a boy in many ways but he had chosen violence as a way of life. What pricked at Powell's conscience was the knowledge the boy came from a family who were all members of the IRA. Had he really had any choice about living a life without violence? It was a recurring thought during the time Powell spent in Ireland.

There was a time Afina would probably have happily shot Stefan or Dimitry but she had recently succeeded in moving on with her life. She had a good job and close friends. Powell was feeling guilty, she was once again being dragged back into a violent world, not of her making. Her continued association with him was putting her life in danger.

There were similarities to his wife's death, which had been the cause of many sleepless nights and guilty feelings. Vanessa had chosen to marry Powell but he had not made her fully aware of his dangerous lifestyle. Just being married to him had been enough to get Vanessa killed. With hindsight he felt he should have left the dangerous world he inhabited behind when he agreed to get married. He had acted selfishly and despite his love for Vanessa, made the wrong choices. He didn't want to repeat the mistake with Afina. He needed to get her to safety, which would be as far away from him as possible.

"Brought some brandy if you're interested?" Powell announced, holding up the bottle and three glasses.

Afina was sat on the sofa and Lara occupied the single armchair. They had immediately stopped talking when they saw him, which made him wonder if he had been the subject of the conversation.

He poured the drinks and handed out the glasses. He thought Afina looked even paler than usual.

"Cheers," Powell toasted and downed his shot in one.

The girls did likewise and he refilled the glasses.

"What have you done with the American?" Afina asked.

"He's safely locked away in the wine cage. Brian's sending someone to collect him. They should be here in about an hour."

"What do we do next?" Afina asked.

"Remember, if the police do ever ask you, you were upstairs in bed and you two can vouch for each other. I was downstairs locking up the bar. That's all you know."

"The man I shot… do you think he will die?" Afina questioned.

"I can't be one hundred per cent certain but I doubt the shot was fatal. It didn't look like you hit any vital organs. He may be in pain and out of work for quite some time but don't lose any sleep over him. He would have killed us without any hint of remorse."

Afina seemed relieved and took a further drink. " I just pointed the gun and pulled the trigger. I'm amazed I even hit him."

"I owe you a big vote of thanks, Afina. You saved my life."

"I did what was necessary."

"You were very brave," Lara added.

"I had no choice. I could not let that man shoot Powell."

"Lara's right," Powell said. "It was brave of you and I'm very grateful."

"Did you learn anything from the American?" Lara asked.

"Nothing very useful. His name is Brown and he is ex CIA. He's a private contractor and he's currently working for a Brit called Barnes. He was brought in to interrogate Al-Hashimi. Seems that's his speciality."

"What sort of person ends up specialising in torture?" Lara was thinking out loud as much as asking a question.

"Sadly, there are plenty of people who enjoy hurting other people. Some of them end up in the army or working for the government. The rest end up as criminals."

"What Powell says is right," Afina added. "I've known men like Victor and Dimitry, who enjoyed hurting people, especially girls."

"What happened to them?" Lara asked.

"Powell killed them both," Afina replied.

Lara looked at Powell but said nothing.

Powell decided he should change the subject. "Afina, I've been thinking and I think it would be a good idea if you go away for a bit. At least until this mess is sorted out."

"This is my home, Powell. I am not running away."

"Powell is probably right," Lara agreed. "I don't want you to get hurt because of me."

"It's nice you are worried for me but I think I've proved I can take care of myself. So I'm staying."

It was too late at night to press the point any further. "We'll talk about it again tomorrow," Powell said. "Right now, I suggest you both get some sleep. We still have to open the bar as usual, tomorrow."

CHAPTER EIGHTEEN

Powell insisted in the morning that Afina should take the day off work despite her protestations. The previous night had been traumatic and Powell wanted her to get away from the bar at least for a few hours, even if she wasn't willing to take a proper holiday. At his suggestion, she agreed to go spend a fun day with Mara, who due to the nature of her work could always be flexible with her time.

Powell was pleased with his small victory. If there was to be any reprisal on the part of Brown's friends, then there was a distinct possibility it would happen very soon. It would be safer for Afina, the farther she was away from the bar or more precisely away from Lara, who currently attracted danger like a magnet. Later in the day, Powell would encourage Afina to stay over at Mara's or with her other friends. He didn't want her returning to the bar for at least twenty four hours.

Once Afina had left, Powell made Jenkins some coffee and they sat down to try and make sense of everything. Powell always found Jenkins made a good sounding board for his ideas. They both came up with various explanations for recent events but each time they also found a flaw in their thinking. They were no nearer understanding why it was so important to kill Lara. Yes, she had seen Al-Hashimi tortured but Powell didn't believe that was enough in itself to require her death.

Lara had undoubtedly stirred the proverbial hornet's nest when she questioned the treatment Al-Hashimi received. By doing so, she had made someone feel threatened and Powell doubted it was just on the level of a slap on the wrist for overzealous interrogation techniques. Someone felt threatened because there was something so important at stake, even the tiniest risk to the operation had to be squashed.

Powell and Jenkins made Lara replay everything that had happened during the interrogation. They especially went over in detail everything Al-Hashimi revealed and everyone she had met during the interrogation. The next target was to be the upcoming Conservative party conference in Blackpool. Brian had already passed this information to the police just in case an attack still went ahead. Al-Hashimi was out of the equation and with security tripled, the assumption up until the previous night's bomb attack, had been that the conference was now safe. That was no longer so certain. There were still terrorists at large.

Powell was of the opinion Lara had seen or heard something that was supposed to remain secret but they were no nearer discovering what that was. As lunchtime approached, they took a well-deserved break.

Phoenix was truly shocked by the bombing of the club in London. The news was saying it was another terrorist atrocity and probably committed by the same people responsible for the marathon bombing. Phoenix had been under the impression Al-Hashimi was captured and being interrogated. Certainly he was no longer at the address where he was supposed to be staying. There had been no announcement about his arrest but that was surely because MI5 would be extracting information.

The bombing at the club suggested Al-Hashimi may have evaded capture. He was a brave and resourceful fighter but too much did not make sense. Where had he found the materials for another bomb? He had only been provided with enough Semtex explosive to make the marathon bomb. Maybe he had improvised. His training would have included instructions on how to make a bomb using the type of chemicals that could be found in normal consumer products, such as household cleaners.

This was the worst possible scenario. There would be heightened security everywhere tomorrow due to the threat posed by Al-Hashimi, which would put his own operation at risk. And there was nothing Phoenix could do. He didn't have any way of contacting Al-Hashimi. It looked like his careful planning had been for nothing.

The only other possible explanation for the bombing was it had been carried out by a different organisation. Maybe not even an Arab based group but some group who hated homosexuals. It seemed too much of a coincidence. It must be Al-Hashimi. He knew for certain there were no other ISIS cells operating in the UK.

And who had telephoned claiming credit for the attack? The news was saying it was ISIS and it could be someone back home taking advantage of the opportunity but normally he would be the one making such a call. It had been his operation and it was highly secret. It wasn't possible to believe

Al-Hashimi could have contacted anyone else in the organisation, if he was on the run. Phoenix's instinct told him something wasn't right but equally last night's attack had been more successful than the London bombing. He would accept the positives and not be too concerned about the truth. Any blow against the enemy was a reason to celebrate.

In any other circumstances, Phoenix would have been proud of what Al-Hashimi had achieved. Phoenix would not let this deter him from his own plan. His attack would still go ahead tomorrow even if it was more risky. Following on so quickly from the London pub bombing, the English would surely soon be crippled with fear.

CHAPTER NINETEEN

Barnes met with his CIA co-conspirator in a small café in Queensway, which served in his opinion, the best breakfast in London. It was a little out of the way, which made it perfect for a clandestine meeting. There was no likelihood of bumping into any of their respective colleagues. It was the same café where they had first met and Crawford had sounded Barnes out with his radical and dangerous idea.

Barnes didn't like Crawford on a personal level, he was too brash and frankly, just too American for Barnes's taste. He also had learned never to trust anyone in the CIA. They would ruthlessly pursue their own agenda and trample all over anyone, including supposed allies, in order to achieve their goals. However, he couldn't fault Crawford's current objectives. They shared the same view about where Britain was headed and what was required to alter course. The only issue for Barnes was whether they could get away with such deception. When Crawford explained there was support for the idea at senior levels in both their governments, the decision to proceed became much easier.

"We've had a hiccup," Crawford admitted. "One of my men was badly injured and Brown was taken prisoner last night."

"Rather more than a hiccup, more a bloody case of pneumonia," Barnes replied. "And the woman is still alive. From what you told me, I thought Brown was better than he's shown."

"He's never let me down before and he did a good job at the club last night."

"That was his work?"

"It certainly was."

"Well he's certainly let you down this time and put both our plan and us personally at risk. On the positive side, he's now in our custody. That damned Powell fellow who captured him, had him picked up by a friend who works for us."

"Well that's a stroke of luck. Can you make the problem go away… permanently?" Crawford asked.

"That won't be easy. They are keeping him somewhere off the grid. The DG knows he can't trust his own organisation. I might be able to find out where they are keeping him but then it will be up to you to sort out your mess."

"Okay, I'll give it some serious thought," Crawford said. "Fortunately, Brown doesn't know very much and you guys tend to be too constrained by your rules, to forcefully extract the little he does know. He certainly isn't going to admit to bombing the gay pub and spend the rest of his life in a British jail."

"He's met me and could identify me. I don't call that *not much*."

"You and your team don't officially exist. If they get close, won't they be told to stop poking their noses where they don't belong?"

"They will but it doesn't mean I like the idea of them trying to find me. Brown needs to be silenced before someone discovers they already have last night's bomber in custody. If that happens the gloves will be off and he will want to make a deal."

"I'll get on the case as soon as I leave here," Crawford promised.

"And the woman?"

"I've replaced Brown with someone who will get the job done today so relax a bit."

"Please don't tell me to relax but I am pleased to hear you have already taken steps to put matters right."

"On another positive note," Crawford continued. "The recent bombings have put terrorism very much back at the top of the agenda for your government. When the next bomb goes off, I don't think there will be any further talk about a reduction in your defence spending or any dissenting voices about what should be your number one priority."

"Yes, I must say the marathon bombing alone has had an excellent impact on the public's thinking. Last night's bombing will have everyone running scared. The public don't want to hear any more talk about cutbacks in defence or scrapping Trident. The PM is even doing better in the polls."

"I know our government is unofficially very happy with the outcome. They were getting very worried about your increasing lack of willpower to be an equal partner in fighting terrorism. That seems to have all changed over the last few days."

"Indeed. No one could have foreseen the result of the Labour party election and the public response to his madcap ideas but that juggernaut seems to have come to a sudden halt. In a time of crisis like this, the public aren't going to vote for someone who says we shouldn't shoot terrorists on sight."

"All the public needed was a reminder of how serious the threat is from the likes of ISIS and we plan to give them further reminders."

"I hope you're right. The Russians have seized the initiative by bombing ISIS in Syria. It's madness we can bomb them in Iraq but not Syria, which is their headquarters."

"By the time we've finished, your public will be clamouring for you to attack ISIS on the ground."

"The majority of people are also demanding stricter controls on our borders. The Prime Minister's plan to help refugees in the camps but not flood the country with them is definitely looking the right policy. He's hand has really been strengthened for his negotiations with the EU about border controls. Even the French and Germans are coming around to his way of thinking. All in all it's looking positive."

"One more terrorist attack and our job should be done."

"I don't want to see too many lives lost," Barnes stressed.

"Can't make an omelette without cracking a few eggs."

"The DG will be asking the Prime Minister to raise the matter of Al-Hashimi with your President."

"Relax. There is no record of Al-Hashimi in any of our systems, he simply doesn't exist. We'll just say you've got your wires crossed."

"Is he still providing useful information?" Barnes asked.

"Very useful. A long list of contacts for us to pursue. One particularly interesting name keeps cropping up. Someone called Phoenix, who we would very much like to get our hands on."

"What do you plan to do with him when you've finished?"

"He will be disposed of but that's still some time away."

"I would feel a lot happier knowing he wasn't still alive. It's a risk we don't need to take. He's served his purpose."

"He's too valuable to dispose of yet. Anyway, we plan on him taking the blame for what we're about to do so he needs to remain alive until then."

"That was all well and good before your recent cockups. Having denied his existence we can hardly do a Lazarus with him."

"Don't start getting cold feet now," Crawford warned. "There's no turning back. I said the man we have in custody can take responsibility. We can give him a new name and back story. It won't be Al-Hashimi but another Arab with a history of terrorism. Al-Hashimi only exists as a figment of Lara Saliba's imagination."

"I just don't like all the loose ends. The woman and Brown both need silencing as soon as possible." Barnes found the American very gung-ho in his attitude. He was willing to take far too many risks. When Barnes ran an operation he kept things tight.

CHAPTER TWENTY

Phoenix had spent every waking moment training the other two jihadists. They were young and lacked experience but their devotion was not in doubt. Phoenix would be proud to die alongside such men. If the cancer was not so far advanced, it would be different. He had spent his life fighting in the name of Allah and soon it would be his time to die. It would be a good death, much better than slowly rotting away as the cancer spread throughout his body. It was fitting that his death would help destroy the cancer that pervaded Western countries.

Phoenix's accomplices were young and becoming more impatient with the passing of each day. He had seen their kind many times before, eager to secure their place in Heaven through martyrdom. They would deserve their seventy two virgins when they reached Paradise.

Phoenix was no less excited. If their attack was a success, the shock would reverberate around the world. He was confident the young jihadists would not let him down but there was an element of luck involved, he could not control. Their target was due to be in the conference centre for a particular debate this morning but if he awoke feeling ill and didn't turn up, there was nothing they could do. The attack must go ahead whether he was present or not. There could be no turning back once they entered the centre. The results could still be spectacular even if their number one target escaped.

The young Englishmen had made videos explaining the reasons for their actions and condemning the West in general and Britain in particular, for waging illegal wars. The videos would appear all over the internet within a short time of carrying out their mission. Phoenix had not made a video. The impact of two local Englishmen committing the attack would have far more impact on the British psyche than any video by a known terrorist from the Middle East. Anyway, today was not to be the day he met his maker. When his time came he would be remembered by his actions not by his words in a video.

The young Englishmen were from the north of England and had spent a year in Pakistan training for this moment. They would both be wearing the suicide vests packed full of ball bearings to cause the most damage. Phoenix was travelling with them to ensure everything went smoothly. He was not wearing a vest as he was planning to conduct further attacks over the next month. He wasn't armed but he had told the Englishmen he could help by creating a diversion if the need arose. In truth, he was there to ensure the Englishmen didn't lose their nerve and change their minds about going through with the attack.

Phoenix was glad the day had finally arrived. They had all gone to bed excited both by what lay ahead and the news of the pub bombing. It had further stiffened the resolve of the jihadists to complete their mission successfully. They needed to emulate the success of the person responsible for the pub bombing, who they assumed was part of a coordinated campaign of attacks against the English. Phoenix let them believe that was the plan and hid his misgivings.

They were all awake early and said prayers together. Not much was said as the men worked to prepare their vests. The mood was solemn in the house. The robes they wore concealed any signs of the bombs and Phoenix inspected both men to ensure nothing was visible. They would not be comfortable due to the extra weight but to a passerby there was no evidence of their intentions.

At eleven they left the house for the final time and took the tube to Victoria. It was Wednesday morning and a bright, sunny day. A good day to do God's work. The train was almost empty and the three men were easily able to find seats together at a table. Phoenix made no attempt at conversation during the one hour journey. There was nothing more needed to be said. Each of them knew their roles and Phoenix was confident the men would not falter at the last moment.

The train pulled into Brighton station and they exited through the barriers. Phoenix led the way out of the front of the station and they walked downhill towards the seafront. They passed the clock tower and kept walking, barely bothering to notice their surroundings. All that mattered was their destination. They quickly reached the bottom of the road and turned right by the Odeon cinema. They immediately crossed the road so they were by the seafront.

Phoenix looked out to sea and thought of his homeland. As a small child he enjoyed visits to the sea. He was a good swimmer but those days were long gone. At least he had been lucky enough to live a full life. Too many of his country's children were now dead. Soon he would join them in Heaven.

They stood like tourists, taking in the view of the pier and the beach. As they walked slowly along the front they all caught their first glimpse of the Brighton Centre on the other side of the road. It was time for Phoenix to say goodbye.

CHAPTER TWENTY ONE

Afina and Mara had breakfast at Costa's in the Churchill shopping centre. Afterwards, they were planning to go shopping and then in the afternoon maybe see a film.

"Are you sure you don't mind not working today?" Afina asked.

"I've been working hard lately so I deserve some time off. Anyway, the daytime isn't often very busy. My customers are a bit like vampires. They only come out at night."

"What time do you want to go back to work tonight?"

"When we have finished having fun."

"That will be very late then." If their previous nights out together was anything to go by, the evening would almost certainly end in the early hours of the next morning, having drunk a combination of too many cocktails, wine and shots.

"I'm not really bothered about working tonight. I had an overnight last night."

"How was it?"

"He wouldn't let me sleep," Mara smiled. "Not that I am complaining, he paid me eight hundred pounds and it was fun."

"Eight hundred pounds! He must be rich?"

"He has a company that designs web sites. He's become quite a regular."

"I used to have to fuck more than twenty men to make that type of money."

"I'm sure he'd like a threesum if you're interested," Mara teased.

"Very funny," Afina answered.

As manager of Powell's bar, Afina had to work hard for a whole week to earn eight hundred pounds and then, unlike Mara, she would have to pay taxes. She was a little jealous of Mara's income but she would never go back to selling her body.

"You need some excitement," Mara said. "Your life is too boring. Have you fucked that nice waiter yet?"

"I don't like Neill that much," Afina stressed. Mara had tried to persuade her last time they met that she should have pity on him as he so obviously fancied her. "Anyway, I actually have plenty of excitement in my life at the moment. That is why I am with you today."

"What do you mean? What excitement? Have you met someone," Mara probed.

"Excitement doesn't have to involve being with a man."

"Of course not but you will break my heart if you tell me you are in love with some other woman."

"There is no woman or man in my life. At least not in the way you mean."

"Good so there is still hope for me then," Mara teased.

"I am very happy being single."

"I am also happy and single. When you are single is when you are supposed to have fun."

"I have fun."

"Fun includes sex. You still haven't fucked anyone since you stopped working. When you are old and married you will only have sex with one man. Now is the time to enjoy yourself."

"Do you want to know about my excitement or not?" Afina asked, becoming slightly exasperated with Mara.

"Okay so what is this new excitement in your life?".

Afina had always planned to tell Mara about the previous night's events but just been waiting for the right moment. She took five minutes to explain about Lara coming to the bar and everything leading up to shooting the man in the street.

Mara was visibly shocked. "You should have told me first thing, not let me ramble on speaking rubbish."

"So now I have told you."

"I'm so sorry. I have such a big mouth sometimes."

Afina purposefully said nothing. She just smiled.

"You can disagree with me," Mara said after a little time.

"About which bit exactly?"

"Very funny."

"I think you must agree my night was more exciting than your overnight sex with a punter."

"You shouldn't joke about it. You could have been killed."

"Well I wasn't."

"You must come and live with me," Mara quickly offered. "I have the spare bedroom."

"I am happy at the bar. And I can't imagine being in the next bedroom while you are working. I'd never get any sleep."

"But it is dangerous at the bar. What if the men come back?"

"Powell doesn't think they will."

"Powell would want you to stay with me. He wants you to be safe."

"I will be safe," Afina replied.

"You mean you want to be wherever he is but in case you haven't noticed, being near Powell is often dangerous."

"Perhaps you are right but I feel safe when I am with Powell. He has saved my life on more than one occasion. And it is this Lara woman who has caused the trouble not Powell."

"And now you have saved his life. You are even."

"Mara, do you forget, his daughter is dead because of me. We can never be even. Now, enough of this talk. I am supposed to be having fun today."

Mara smiled. "Sorry, it's just that I care for you and worry about you. I am going to buy you a present today."

"You don't have to. I have my own money."

"Yes but I want to buy my best friend a present so drink up and let's go shopping. And afterwards, I think we should do something mad. Let's go on the pier and sit on that terrible ride, which will scare us to death. At least, it will scare me to death."

CHAPTER TWENTY TWO

Phoenix watched as the two men crossed the road and walked towards the conference centre. It was a moment he had dreamed about for many years. A long journey was reaching its conclusion. There would be strict security checks but both men had the correct passes. Fortunately, obtaining security clearance had been quite easy, especially as the Labour party was welcoming many new members since the election of their new leader. It would have been impossible for Phoenix to get a pass but for two working class young men, from the north of England, with no criminal history, it was quite easy.

They had spent months in preparation and Phoenix said a silent prayer it was not a wasted effort. This was an opportunity to strike at the English political system not just the public. Killing a former Prime Minister, who was responsible for the invasion of Iraq, would strike fear into all politicians. It was proof no one was safe from the long reach of ISIS. There was also a good chance of killing some of the others who had been in government at the time.

His comrades back home had been dubious about the plan, reminding him there would be a heavy security presence. Far better, they suggested, to attack a shopping mall, cinema or football stadium in the centre of London. Phoenix though would not be denied. The potential prize was too great. Despite the many attacks in the West, there had never been a single instance of killing a member of government, let alone a former Prime Minister. He had won the argument and now the day had arrived. He prayed he would be proved correct.

As the two men reached the conference centre, they turned in towards the entrance and at that point they were lost from Phoenix's sight. He turned away and started to walk back the way he had come. He had not gone far when a deafening explosion sounded from the direction of the centre. It was quickly followed by a second explosion. He cursed and looked back down the road to see smoke billowing into the air.

What had gone wrong? There had not been time for them to have made it inside the conference centre. Had they been searched and the bombs discovered? He could only hope their sacrifice had not been in vain. At the least they must have killed the policemen on guard and the security staff. He couldn't risk getting closer to check. Already, people were rushing in his direction, desperately trying to get away from the explosions in case there were further bombs.

He could see that cars were strewn across the road in front of the entrance to the centre. The bombs had cut a swathe through the traffic and people were emerging from cars grasping at their injuries, looking for help. It was chaos and Phoenix decided he had a small window before the area was flooded with police. He jogged towards the centre, ignoring the shouts of people running in his direction, warning him of the danger.

He twice shouted he was a doctor and as he came close to the centre he could see nothing but devastation. A policeman lay on the ground with his insides spilling out onto the pavement. Beside him lay a Heckler & Koch MP5 submachine gun, which appeared undamaged. He knelt beside the policeman and pretended to be administering first aid. He slid the gun towards himself and covered it with his robe. Then he reached down and through the pocket of his robe he took hold of the weapon. He took some spare ammunition and placed it in his other pocket. He stood back up and looked around. It may not have been a complete success but there were still a substantial number of casualties.

"You, what are you doing," a man in a suit shouted, who had appeared from inside the building.

"I'm a doctor but I'm afraid this man is beyond help." Phoenix turned his back on the man and started to walk away. He was worried he would attract attention just by his Arab looks and clothes.

Sirens could be heard approaching but still there was only chaos everywhere. Phoenix found it impossible to properly conceal the gun beneath his garment. He was grasping it through the pocket in his robe, holding the gun pointing down by the side of his body.

He was walking quickly and had arrived back by the cinema. He looked around, uncertain which direction to take. He could return to London as per the original plan but then he wouldn't be able to keep the weapon. He liked the idea of dying with a weapon in his hand. He would take many of the enemy with him and the shock would reverberate around this God forsaken country, hopefully demonstrating to others, who would follow in his footsteps, it was possible to strike at the heart of the enemy.

If Al-Hashimi was still free to carry out further attacks, then Phoenix was not needed. The illness was getting worse and soon he would be too weak to plan further attacks. He did not want to die in pain or unable to look after himself with his memory failing. It was not a fit way for a warrior to die.

He was decided, the only question was where to make his last stand. He noticed the pier sticking out into the sea and thought it would make a good place to die. With its narrow entrance it would also be a difficult place for people to escape. They would be trapped and he was sure he could kill many before he died. His death would make a good headline in tomorrow's newspapers.

Phoenix crossed the road to be once again next to the seafront. Policemen were running past him heading for the conference center. Members of the public were standing around asking anyone walking from the direction of the explosion, if they knew what had happened. Phoenix kept his head down and avoided the questions.

He smiled and knew he had made the right decision. He had always thought he would die with a gun in his hand. At last that would be proved true.

CHAPTER TWENTY THREE

Afina and Mara finished shopping and discussed what they would have for lunch. Afina suggested fish and chips and Mara readily agreed. As they wanted to visit the pier later anyway, they decided it would also be a good spot for lunch. Halfway along the pier was a restaurant, where they had eaten before, which exclusively sold traditional fish and chips. Afina had been introduced to the idea of having vinegar on her chips, which she now loved.

Despite the pleasant weather, the pier wasn't very busy. Most people with normal jobs were at work and all but the youngest children were at school. They sat inside the restaurant rather than have a takeaway so they could enjoy a drink. The young male waiter was eyeing up both girls as he took their order for drinks. As usual, Mara encouraged the attention.

After lunch, they planned to try all the rides. One in particular was very scary and Mara joked she was in need of some Dutch courage. She had refused to try it the last time they visited the pier but today she had promised she would be braver. Afina enjoyed the scary rides and loved poking fun at Mara's discomfort. As Afina was comfortable doing somersaults and back flips, a few twists and turns on a fairground ride were a piece of cake.

They ordered a bottle of dry white wine and it had just been served when they heard the two massive explosions in quick succession. Everyone in the restaurant looked at each other, seeking an explanation for what they had heard. A couple of people ran towards the doors, intent on checking what had happened.

"What the hell was that?" Afina asked.

"I'm not sure. It sounded like a bomb."

"A bomb! Do you think it could be the bar?" Afina asked in a panic.

"It sounded too near to be someone blowing up the bar."

Afina reached for her phone and dialled Powell. "Is everything okay?" she immediately asked, when he answered. "Did you hear the explosion?"

"It sounded like a bomb but it wasn't anywhere near us," Powell confirmed.

"Thank God."

"Hang on, I've just turned the news on. They're saying something about it. They think someone just tried to bomb the Labour Party conference. Are you all right? Where are you?"

"Yes we're fine. We're on the pier having lunch, although we haven't actually ordered any food yet. What should we do?"

"I'd come straight back to the bar. You can eat here. It's going to get chaotic in town."

"Okay, we won't be long." Afina ended the call and turned to Mara. "Powell thinks we should get out of town. Do you want to come back to the bar?"

"Let's have some of the wine first," Mara suggested, raising her glass. "You do attract trouble," she laughed. "I spend one day with you and look what happens."

"Well, I'm not sure about which of us causes the most trouble. I had a very quiet life in Romania before I met you."

Mara looked serious for a moment. "I'm really sorry for everything that has happened to you, Afina."

"Don't be silly, it wasn't your fault. You're my best friend. And you almost died saving my life."

"But everything you've endured was because of my family. I feel very guilty sometimes."

"Well in that case you can pay for the wine."

They explained to the waiter they were leaving without food because of the bombing and after a few minutes they had paid the bill and were ready to leave.

Several of the diners had now left their seats and ventured outside, encouraged by one of the earlier men to leave, who had excitedly rushed back in, telling everyone there had been a terrorist attack. The staff were animatedly discussing what had happened and seemed to have forgotten about serving.

As soon as they left the restaurant they could see the plume of smoke in the distance. They leaned against the railing and looked across the sea towards the Conference Centre.

"I wonder how many people have been killed," Mara said.

"It looks bad," Afina replied. "I didn't think anyone would ever bomb

Brighton."

"Why is the world so full of evil men," Mara said. "My family are bad enough but even they aren't like these terrorists."

Before Afina could answer there was a series of sharp cracks like firecrackers going off, coming from the entrance to the pier.

"What was that?" Afina asked.

"I think it was gunshots. What should we do?"

"Quickly, we need to get away from here," Afina said, taking hold of Mara's hand. She started pulling her away from the further sound of gunshots, hurrying towards the end of the pier.

CHAPTER TWENTY FOUR

Powell put the phone down on Afina and returned to watching the news. An eye witness was reporting how his car was thrown across the road and crashed into an oncoming car. He had been lucky all the traffic was going slowly at the time of the bomb because of the traffic lights up ahead having just turned red.

Powell flicked through a few channels. There were no shortage of cameras and news reporters already covering the explosions as there had been hundreds of reporters in town to cover the conference.

The phone rang again and this time it was Brian.

"When I first heard there was a bomb in Brighton, I was certain it would be your bar," Brian said. "I had quite a shock until someone explained it was at the Labour conference."

"Didn't know you cared," Powell joked.

"Not about you but I do care for Afina. I have a horrible, nagging doubt that somehow it's not a coincidence. This must have something to do with Lara and Al-Hashimi."

"I think we can again safely assume the bomber wasn't Al-Hashimi as someone has hold of him. And according to Lara, he said the next target was the Conservative conference so it seems he didn't know about last night's bomb or this one. That means there is another cell operating completely independently of Al-Hashimi."

"Today's bombs were set off by two suicide bombers so a different modus operandi to the other attacks."

"It was lucky they detonated outside the conference centre and didn't get inside."

"There are metal detectors, like at the airports, you have to walk through to enter so they wouldn't be able to get past them with a bomb. They are a new addition this year so someone made a good decision."

"They might not have realised that. So what's the news on Brown?"

"Brown has just been released."

"How is that possible?" Powell asked, shocked.

"The Americans vouched for him. Said he was working for them and assured us the man they have interrogated isn't called Al-Hashimi and had nothing to do with the Marathon bombing. They say he was a terrorist suspect they have been pursuing for a long time."

"Forgive me if I'm feeling slightly incredulous. Does the DG actually believe that bullshit?"

"I said it was the official version. The DG has to keep the Americans sweet and isn't entirely sure what to believe. He doesn't trust the Yanks but he relies on their cooperation. And there is no trace of Al-Hashimi. No one has admitted knowing the name. We only have Lara's word that the man even exists."

"How does the DG explain the attempts on Lara's life?"

"An overzealous Brown not entirely understanding his remit… The CIA trying to cover their tracks… It doesn't matter. The Americans will get a severe slap on the wrist but that's becoming a regular occurrence."

Powell was almost speechless. "Someone needs reminding this is the UK not the wild west."

"I agree but we are very reliant on the Americans for intel so our partnership with them is by no means equal."

"Do you think this means Lara is safe?" Right now she and Jenkins were back at his house.

"Difficult to know."

"Surely Brown wouldn't dare try anything now?"

"Brown is on the next plane back to the States. I can't say that categorically means she's safe but the Americans will have a lot of uncomfortable questions to answer if anything happens to Lara. Problem is that's not always enough to keep them under control…And they have no shortage of the likes of Brown to do their dirty work."

Powell froze as he heard the television news. "I have to go," he interrupted Brian. "The news is reporting there's been some shooting on the pier. Afina's having lunch there with Mara. I need to make sure they are all right."

He ended the call and immediately tried to call Afina. The call went straight to voice mail. He left a message asking her to phone him back urgently. Then he called Mara with the same result.

They should have been back at the bar by now if they had left straight away, as he suggested. Maybe they had difficulty getting a taxi. The roads would be chaotic. Or perhaps they were still on the pier when the terrorists attacked. He needed to get to the pier. If they returned while he was looking for them, the bar staff could call and let him know they were safe.

Customers in the bar had left their tables and were crowding around the television to hear the news. He found one of the reliable waiters and told her he was going out and wasn't sure when he would be back. She was in charge until he returned. She looked uncertain but he told her he had every confidence in her and she could call him if there was an emergency. He also stressed she was to call if Afina turned up.

Next, he hurried to his office and collected his gun. It seemed to have seen a great deal of use recently, given it had previously sat for so many years unused in his safe. He walked at his fastest pace out of the bar, trying not to run.

Once on the street he stepped halfway into the middle of the road to flag down a taxi. The driver had no choice but to stop and initially wasn't keen to head towards the pier but Powell persuaded him with a fistful of money, telling him somewhere close would be fine.

Powell called Afina twice more but each time the call went unanswered. He found Mara's number but the result was the same. Why the hell was neither of them answering? He could only think of one reason and it made him feel sick in his stomach. He told the driver to go faster. If it had been a normal day, Afina would have been working in the bar and safe. Why the hell did he persuade her to take a day off? Was life trying to laugh in his face yet again.

The taxi journey took only ten minutes and he ran the last hundred metres. Police had already cordoned off the entrance to the pier. There was chaos everywhere as people who had gathered to find out what was happening were being told in no uncertain terms, to leave the area as quickly as possible as there may be further terrorists.

Once people got the message they started running in all directions and Powell was the only person still trying to get to the pier.

A bulky police officer spied him and put his large frame directly in front of him. "You need to move away, sir," the officer said forcefully.

"My friends are on the pier…"

"It wasn't a request," the officer shouted. "Go home and wait to hear from them."

Still Powell didn't move. "Are there terrorists on the pier?" he asked.

"Please move away, sir or I will be forced to arrest you."

"Just tell me if there are fucking terrorists on the pier," Powell demanded.

"This is your final warning, sir. Move away now."

Powell could see the officer wasn't going to be helpful. He was of a mature age, which suggested he had been passed over for promotion more than once. He was overweight and had a tired look, like he had seen it all before. He had probably heard every excuse ever invented. He would stand where he was told all day if necessary and no one would get past.

Powell had a strong urge to simply knock him to the ground. It wasn't a good idea. There were too many of his colleagues in close vicinity. The presence of so many police, and more were arriving every second, must mean one or more terrorists were indeed on the pier. At least there was no immediate sound of gunfire. Then he realised that could be because everyone was already dead.

CHAPTER TWENTY FIVE

Afina and Mara ran towards the end of the pier, to get away from the gunshots but without any idea of what they would do once they reached the end.

They stood breathless by all the amusement rides. Afina noticed the ghost train and wondered if it might make a good hiding place. There were few options for hiding. Other people were anxiously stood about not knowing what to do. Bizarrely, the Dodgems were still running and a few people were crashing cars into each other, oblivious of the imminent danger.

Afina took a look over the side of the pier. It seemed a very long way down to the sea.

"We may have to jump," Afina suggested.

Mara looked over the side, then back at Afina. "You have to be fucking joking. I'm not jumping down there. I can hardly even swim."

"It will be okay. The waves are not too strong today and I am a good swimmer. Anyway, it is only a last resort."

"Please don't make me jump."

"Honestly, it will be okay. I remember Powell telling me people do it all the time."

"We come from Bucharest not Brighton. You know there is no sea in Bucharest. I was never taken swimming when I was growing up and I'm not an athlete like you. I come from a family of gangsters not swimmers."

"Just trust me. It's better than getting shot."

There was the sound of further shots and they were definitely getting closer. Suddenly a group of people came running towards them from the direction of the shots. People were screaming and there was no doubt they were trying to get away from whoever was doing the shooting.

In the distance Afina could see a man in Arab clothing walking slowly towards where she was standing. He had a gun and was casually shooting at anyone he saw but most people were now crowded at the end of the pier. He was advancing and Afina knew many people would end up dead if they stayed where they were.

"Anyone who knows how to swim must jump in to the sea," she shouted at everyone. "We must jump now or he'll kill us all."

A couple of people looked over the side of the pier as if considering the prospect. Most people were crouching behind the various fun fair rides.

"Mara, we need to jump now." Then seeing her reluctance, Afina added, "Unless you have a better idea?"

"I can't. You jump, Afina. He can't shoot all of us."

"We'll do it together." Afina held out her hand.

The terrorist was now clearly within sight. Afina looked at him and he smiled. She shivered and half dragged Mara away from his view.

"Quickly, come with me," Afina demanded, still pulling on Mara's hand.

Afina led the way to the other side of the pier. She spotted a lifesaving ring attached to the wall and yanked it away. She was about to put it over Mara's head when she noticed a mother and young child approach.

"Are you going to jump?" the woman asked.

"We must all jump or be shot," Afina answered.

"Please take my child," the mother implored.

Afina knew she had only thirty seconds to escape. "Here take this ring," she said, thrusting it at the woman. "Put it over your head, climb over the side and I'll pass you your daughter." Afina thought the little girl was about three years old.

"Thank you," the woman replied and started climbing over the side.

When the woman was ready Afina took the daughter from her pushchair. "We're all going to have some great fun now," Afina said to the girl, as she handed her to the mother.

"I don't know if I can," the woman said, gripping tightly to her child and looking down to the sea.

"Hold on to your daughter," Afina said and gave the woman a strong push on her shoulder. She disappeared from sight with a scream.

"Our turn," Afina said, turning to Mara.

"I'm not sure…"

Two further shots boomed out and it was evident the gunman was close. Afina climbed the fence and Mara quickly followed.

"In ten minutes we'll be drinking a brandy," Afina promised. "Make sure you hold your breath as you hit the water."

She held out her hand and Mara gripped it tightly. The option for any last second change of mind on Mara's part was removed as Afina jumped off the edge, ensuring she was still holding firmly on to Mara.

"Fuuuuck!" Mara screamed as she dropped.

Afina couldn't hold on to Mara's hand as they fell. As she hit the water, she was covered by the waves and when she surfaced, she immediately looked for Mara. The drop had not been as bad as she had anticipated. She had felt almost as scared as Mara but the feeling was no different to the first time she tried a double somersault.

Afina quickly spotted Mara, frantically splashing her arms around in an attempt to keep her head above water. Afina swam the short distance towards her and as she came near, Mara grabbed for her arm with the result that Afina was temporarily dragged under the waves. She broke free of Mara's grip and shouted at her to stop trying to drown them. Afina held Mara under her arms and forced her onto her back, telling her to keep calm and kick with her legs.

Afina eventually managed to manoeuvre Mara under the pier where there were metal girders to hold. A more relaxed Mara smiled with relief and held on tightly.

"We're safe here," Afina smiled. "We can't be seen from the pier."

"That was the scariest thing I've ever done," Mara replied, excitedly.

"We can try it again another day, just for fun," Afina suggested.

"No fucking chance."

Afina was looking around, trying to spot the mother with the young girl. She saw them a few metres away from the side of the pier. In the same moment she was relieved to see them safe, she heard another gunshot and saw the water splash close to the rubber ring. The woman screamed out and tried to shield her child.

Afina swam a couple of metres to the side of the pier and saw the terrorist leaning over the side, pointing his gun at the woman and child.

"Leave them alone you bastard," she shouted, trying to attract the terrorist's attention.

He saw Afina waving her arms and immediately fired in her direction. Afina took a deep breath and dived underwater. She swam towards the woman, remaining underwater. She surfaced about a metre from the ring and took hold of the towing rope. She held it firmly and began swimming back to the pier. The terrorist fired a further shot which missed and Afina breathed a huge sigh of relief once she was safely back under the protection of the pier.

"Thank you so much," the mother said. "That was very brave of you."

Afina just smiled and turned towards Mara. "I'm going to take these guys to the shore, then I'll come back for you."

"I'm not going anywhere."

Afina pulled the ring as she swam, careful to keep within the cover of the pier. As she neared the end of the pier she could see people gathered on the beach.

CHAPTER TWENTY SIX

Powell was looking out towards the pier when he spotted someone he recognised.

"That man will vouch for me," Powell said, pointing at the firearms officer, who a year earlier had been in charge of breaking into Stefan's house, albeit Powell had ended up going in ahead of the police. It was the day Mara had been shot and almost killed. It wasn't a day he would ever forget. What was his bloody name? "Hey," he shouted and waved at the officer.

The police officer blocking his path turned to see the direction Powell was pointing. Powell used the opportunity of his being distracted to push past and managed to get a few metres before he felt his arm gripped from behind.

"Where do you think you're going?" the policeman asked sternly. "I've just about had enough of you."

Powell once again resisted the temptation to throw the policeman to the floor and settled for shouting again at the officer he recognised.

The officer finally realised someone was trying to get his attention and slowly his expression went from a lack of understanding to recognition. He walked briskly towards Powell.

"Powell isn't it? What brings you here?"

"Afina and Mara are on the pier. They were the two girls you helped rescue last year."

The officer turned towards his colleague. "I'll handle it from here, thanks."

The policeman walked away with a disgruntled look.

"Sorry, I don't remember your name," Powell apologised.

"DI Dan Simmons. Look, I've only got a second. We're about to move down the pier and check the situation."

"Are people still alive on the pier?"

"Powell, I honestly have no idea. We don't know how many gunmen there are or how many civilians may be dead or alive."

"I don't suppose you'd let me on the pier, Dan."

"Sorry, not this time. I promise to let you know as soon as I know something."

"Afina!" Powell suddenly shouted. He could see her emerge from under the pier, pulling a woman and child to safety. He immediately sprinted towards her, closely followed by Simmons.

Other officers were rushing to aid the woman and child as Afina turned back towards the sea.

"Afina, wait. It's me," Powell shouted as he came near to her.

She turned and smiled as she realised who was calling her name. "Powell, I have to go back for Mara. She can't swim." She was breathing heavily from her exertions.

Powell grabbed hold of Afina by the arm. "Where is she?"

"Underneath the pier, towards the end."

"Simmons, you look after Afina. I'll go get Mara." Powell started to throw off his clothes.

Afina looked ready to argue but Simmons said, "Afina, you've done more than your bit. Let Powell get Mara and I need you to tell me everything you know about the situation on the pier. How many gunmen are there?"

"I saw just one."

"Does he have explosives? I mean, is he wearing a suicide vest?"

"I don't know. I didn't see anything but I couldn't be one hundred per cent certain."

"How many people are there on the pier?"

"Maybe thirty or forty."

"Come with me," Simmons said. "You need to brief my men. And we need to get you out of those wet clothes."

Afina was shaking from the extremely cold sea but didn't move. "I promised Mara I'd go back for her."

"Afina, I'm a stronger swimmer than you and you need to go help Simmons," Powell said firmly.

He was down to his boxers and didn't wait to debate the matter any further. He ran towards the sea and braced himself for what he knew was going to be freezing water. As he dived in

Other officers were taking care of the woman and child. They were wrapping them in blankets.

"She saved our lives," the woman said, as she came level with Simmons.

"It was nothing," Afina answered.

"What's your name?" the woman asked.

"Afina."

"Thank you, Afina. I can never repay you for what you've done." She leaned towards Afina and gave her a large hug. "I'm Julie and this is Sara."

"Let's go get you some dry clothes and a hot drink," one of the female officers accompanying Julie said. "We don't want you dying of pneumonia after what you've been through."

CHAPTER TWENTY SEVEN

Powell had returned with Mara without further incident. She was shivering and in danger of suffering from hypothermia as he helped her up the beach so he was pleased to see paramedics waiting with blankets. Several others were also emerging from the sea, having followed Afina's lead and jumped from the pier.

Powell picked up his clothes from the beach and followed the paramedics to a nearby ambulance. The water had been freezing cold and he smiled at the thought it was the first time in over twenty years he'd been swimming in Brighton's sea. He often swam for fitness in one of the local pools but swimming in the sea was saved for very warm climates.

Mara was taken inside the back of the ambulance but was protesting she didn't need to go to hospital. She wanted a large brandy and to see Afina. Powell also declined the invitation to visit hospital for a check-up. He used the blanket as a makeshift towel and dressed, sitting in the front of the ambulance to remove his wet boxers and put on his jeans.

Then he informed the para medics he was going shopping for essentials and would be back as quickly as possible. He hurried to nearby East Street and went in the first female fashion shop. He grabbed the first young, assistant he saw and told her what he urgently needed. Fifteen minutes later he was back at the beach with two bags full of clothes. He found Afina talking to Mara and handed each of them a bag of clothes.

He left them to get changed in the back of the ambulance and when they emerged, he thought the shop assistant had done a pretty good job of choosing clothes. His instructions had been to buy two sets of clothes she would personally like to wear. He omitted to mention the help he'd received when the girls praised his choices.

"Has Simmons finished with you?" Powell asked Afina.

"Yes, he and his men are on the pier now. I hope they kill that bastard terrorist. I can't believe how he was shooting at women and children. He seemed to be enjoying himself."

"How many people were still on the pier when you jumped?"

"I'm not sure. Probably about thirty. I don't understand why more of them didn't jump."

"I wouldn't have jumped if I'd been by myself," Mara answered. "You made me do it."

Powell smiled at the thought of Afina forcing Mara to jump. "I suggest we retire to the bar for some refreshments and food. I need a drink. The pair of you scared me to death when you didn't answer your phones."

"We were a bit busy," Afina smiled. "Can we stay around a bit longer and find out what happens to all of the people on the pier?"

"If it ends up as a hostage situation, it could go on for many hours. We can follow events on the news. It's being broadcast live."

"Sounds good to me," Mara replied. "I'm starving but mostly I need a very large drink."

"Okay, that makes sense," Afina agreed." And I must admit I'm hungry as well."

Powell took his phone from his pocket. "I think I'll give Jenkins a call and tell him to bring Lara to the bar. I think we deserve something of a celebration."

"I hope they can get our bags back from the pier," Afina said, turning to Mara. "It has all our money, our phones, keys, everything."

"I need to get very drunk," Mara said. "And as I don't have any money or cards, right now I'm very happy that Powell owns a bar."

Powell tried a couple of times to call both Jenkins and Lara without success. "That's strange. Neither of them are answering. Let's grab a taxi and make a detour by my place to see what they're up to."

"You don't think they're in trouble" Afina asked.

"I'm sure there's an innocent explanation. I'll keep trying them." Powell could think of one explanation why both their phones might be unavailable. He knew Jenkins had always fancied Lara and wondered if perhaps they had taken their friendship to a new level.

CHAPTER TWENTY EIGHT

Powell left the girls in the taxi while he walked up the path to his house. He reasoned if there was a problem, the taxi driver could get them to safety. He knew there was trouble as he came close enough to see the front door was ajar. He hurried back down the path and opened the rear door of the taxi.

"I'll see you back at the bar," Powell informed the girls. "There's a couple of things I need to do first. Get some drinks in and we'll all be there soon."

"Is there a problem?" Afina asked. "We can wait for you."

"There's no problem and anyway, we can't all fit in one taxi."

Powell gave the driver the name of the bar and handed Afina enough money to cover the fare. Then he closed the taxi door and watched it pull away.

He retraced his steps up the path. He listened at the front door but there was no sound from within the house, which was in itself surprising. Jenkins always had the radio and television on, wherever he was staying.

Powell slowly pushed the door open. "Jenkins... Lara," he called out. "Anyone at home?"

He stepped inside the house but left the front door open in case he should need to make a speedy exit. He wished he was armed.

He stood at the bottom of the stairs and shouted, "Is anyone up there?" He didn't want to walk in on them having sex but that now seemed even more unlikely. They wouldn't have left the front door open.

He opened the door to his right, which led to the lounge. No sign of anyone and no indication of anything out of place. He returned to the hallway and this time took the door to the left which led to the large kitchen and dining room. Again there was no sign of trouble.

The study at the end of the hallway was similarly undisturbed and he began to think his imagination was getting the better of his common sense. They had probably just got bored at home and gone out into town, forgetting to close the front door properly. That didn't explain why neither of them was answering their phones.

At the bottom of the stairs, he thought he heard a sound coming from upstairs. He stayed still and the noise was repeated. A definite sound coming from the main bedroom. It was a squeaking noise like bed springs moving. Perhaps they were having sex after all and were so involved they hadn't heard him call out. He took the stairs on the balls of his feet but they were old and still creaked.

On the upstairs landing he stood outside his bedroom for a few seconds and listened. He was very unsure what he was going to find within but decided the time for subtlety was past. He threw open the door and sprung inside, ready to engage any intruders.

Jenkins was lying on the bed with his hands tied behind his back and his legs tied together at the ankles. There was something stuffed in his mouth, making it impossible to speak but what held Powell's attention was the rope tied around Jenkins neck and leading to the headboard. It was a noose and if he moved away from the headboard it tightened. Powell could see it was making inroads into Jenkins neck, caused probably by his attempts to move his body to attract attention.

Powell rushed back down the stairs and returned with a large and very sharp kitchen knife. He cut the various ropes holding Jenkins in place, who then removed a pair of Powell's boxers from his mouth.

"Where's Lara?" Powell asked.

"They took her. She's alive. They could have killed us both if they wanted but they didn't."

Powell was relieved a little by that news. "What happened?"

"Delivery of a parcel. I was in the kitchen. Lara opened the door before I could say anything. Two men grabbed her and pushed their way into the house before I could respond. I came out of the kitchen to find two guns pointed at me. I'm sorry. She shouldn't have opened the bloody door without checking with me first."

"Like you said, if they had wanted her dead they would have just killed her. I'm a bit surprised they didn't shoot you."

"Might have been preferable to having your underwear stuffed halfway down my throat."

"At least they were clean."

"I guess there orders were not to shoot anyone unless absolutely necessary."

"Anything distinctive about them?"

"They were professionals and they both had American accents."

"Americans again. Let's go back to the bar and discuss what we do next. By the way, when did all this happen?"

"They came about ten thirty."

"Three hours ago. So you don't know there's been a terrorist attack in Brighton?"

"What's happened?"

"I'll tell you all about it in the taxi."

CHAPTER TWENTY NINE

Barnes telephoned Crawford and insisted they meet immediately. It was early evening and he needed a drink. Thirty minutes later they were sitting in a secluded corner of the Mayfair club.

"It's been quite a day," Barnes said. "Was this your work?"

"God no. We aren't organised yet."

"I hope you're telling me the bloody truth… So if it wasn't you, who the hell was it?"

"Good question."

"Has Al-Hashimi intentionally misled us? He said the plan was to hit the Conservative conference in Blackpool. Was he lying?"

"I guarantee he wasn't lying. No one can go through what he did and not tell the truth. I fear there must have been a second cell operating, which Al-Hashimi knew nothing about."

"So you think the plan was to hit both conferences?" Barnes asked, not sounding convinced.

"It looks that way. On the plus side, someone is doing our job for us. Almost fifty people dead including those shot on the pier. Today won't be forgotten quickly."

"I don't share your excitement at the thought of so many people killed," Barnes responded. "And we were lucky it wasn't many more."

"Casualties of war."

"These were members of the public not soldiers fighting a war."

"We're all fighting this war in case you hadn't noticed. Nine eleven we lost almost three thousand civilians."

"Back to the present. With what's happened today it doesn't really seem necessary to go ahead with any further attacks. The outrage is already at maximum level."

"Our plans are too far advanced to halt now. Anyway, there's no harm in ramping up the pressure. We can't afford for this to be all forgotten in a few months when we need you guys on board with putting ground forces in to Syria."

"I wouldn't have thought we were essential anymore. The Russians, French and you guys are bombing the hell out of ISIS in Syria."

"With the support of the Russians, Assad is winning the war against ISIS. Having won the war, at some point he will invite ground forces to help establish the peace. You don't want to be left out in the cold. We can't have the Russians taking the lead role in determining the future of the Assad regime."

"I broadly agree but the main reason we agreed to work with you on this operation is to reverse the terrible decline in spending on our security. We are in favour of bombing ISIS in Syria but ground forces is a whole different matter."

"We can't have half measures this time around. We need to put an end to ISIS."

"I hear what you say but sadly, ISIS isn't going anywhere no matter what steps we take. What we need is to massively invest in detecting and preventing terrorism."

"We plan to wipe them off the face of the earth. The Russians and French feel the same way."

"Let's get back to the present. Brown is on the way back to the States. What will you do with him?"

"He'll be deployed somewhere well out of the way for the immediate future."

"This morning you said if I found where he was being held you'd deal with the problem."

"And I have dealt with it. You couldn't locate him so I decided the best option was to demand his immediate return. We have a job for Brown, then he is likely to meet with an unfortunate accident."

"We still need to deal with the woman."

"We picked her up earlier today."

"You did? Why didn't you tell me?" Barnes asked with a broad smile.

"I'm telling you now. You said we needed to move quickly and we did."

"What do you mean you picked her up?" Barnes asked. "I thought the idea was simply to silence her."

"I have given the matter more thought and decided she can be an invaluable part of our plans. Originally we were going to use Al-Hashimi as the scapegoat for our actions but that idea's gone down the tube. Who would make a better terrorist than a half Arabic woman, who has been radicalised. Perhaps you can build some back story to support the idea?"

Barnes smiled in appreciation. "I do believe you have come up with an excellent solution. It will also explain why she's been running around trying to divert blame towards Al-Hashimi. When do you move ahead with the next step?"

"By this time next week we can be toasting our success."

"I'll pay for the champagne," Barnes promised.

"Sounds good to me."

CHAPTER THIRTY

Powell and Jenkins arrived back at the bar to find Afina and Mara drinking wine and celebrating their escape.

"Did you hear the news?" Afina asked. Then quickly added, "Where's Lara?"

"She's been taken," Powell answered. "I found Jenkins tied up back at the house."

"Who's taken her?" Afina asked.

"We don't know," Jenkins replied. "But they had American accents."

"Shit!" Afina swore.

"What's the news from the pier?" Powell asked.

Mara answered first. "The terrorist is dead. Seems he ran out of ammunition but saved the last bullet for himself."

"Pity," Powell said. "The authorities would have liked to interrogate him."

"I'd have bloody liked to interrogate him," Mara said. "I'd have cut his balls off for making me jump in that water."

Everyone laughed.

"What are we going to do about Lara?" Afina asked. "I don't like her but I hope she's all right."

"They could have killed her at the house," Jenkins replied. "But they didn't so they obviously need her alive for some reason."

"Have you spoken to Brian?" Afina asked.

"On the way over here, " Powell answered. "He says they've released the American we captured. Seems they had no choice."

Afina's face turned pale. "Could he be responsible for kidnapping Lara?"

"Not directly. He was put on a plane back to the States early this morning."

"So what are we going to do next?"

"Jenkins and I are going up to London shortly to meet with Brian and we have just one lead we can pursue to try and get Lara back. Afina, can you hold the fort here?"

"Of course. What are you going to do?"

"We're going to pay a visit to the Mayfair club."

Powell decided to visit the club by himself. He wanted to appear interested in joining rather than arrive in a threatening group. It was just after six when he walked into the club. He couldn't help but be immediately impressed by the opulent surroundings. He'd heard of exclusive clubs for the rich and famous but it was his first time inside one. Everything about the place cried out *establishment*.

There was a small desk in the hallway to greet members and keep out any unwanted visitors. Beyond the desk was a circular hallway with a large stone staircase leading to the next floor. There were paintings on the walls of various important men from history. He smiled at the absence of any pictures of women. This was definitely a club for gentlemen.

Powell had dressed in a smart suit and tie to try and not look out of place in the club. He approached the man behind the desk, who looked up and smiled. He carried himself well and Powell suspected there was every chance he had once served in the armed forces or possibly the police.

"Can I help you, sir?" the man asked politely.

"I hope you can. I was thinking of joining your club. A friend of mine has recommended you and as I was in the area, I thought I'd drop in and see if it's possible to take a look around?"

"Have you filled out the membership application, sir?"

"Not yet, it's a bit early for that. Need to see if it's the right sort of place first. Although from what my friend tells me, it does seem like an excellent establishment."

"And may I ask the name of your friend?"

"Mr. Barnes. We're in the same line of work. He's not here now by any chance, is he? He could show me around the place."

"I'm really not sure, sir. We have hundreds of members. You could try calling his mobile."

Powell took out his mobile without hesitation and called Jenkins. After a second he ended the call.

"Went straight to voicemail. Do you have to turn phones off inside the club?" Powell had spotted the sign reminding members not to use phones within the club. He believed the man on the desk was testing him by telling him to call his friend.

"I forgot, sir. We do indeed have a rule against using phones within the club. Mr. Barnes probably has it switched off."

"Do you know what Mr. Barnes looks like?" Powell asked. "Perhaps you could check if he's here?"

"I'm afraid I can't leave my desk, sir. By the way, I didn't catch your name?"

"Brown."

"That's odd. You don't look like the previous Mr. Brown."

"I'm his replacement."

"Well, sir, I suggest you call the membership secretary, who I am sure will be more than pleased to arrange a visit to view the club." The man looked down at his desk, signalling the conversation was at an end.

Powell didn't see much point in continuing to stand in front of the desk. Perhaps it had been a mistake to give his name as Brown but he had hoped the name would get him to meet Barnes.

There was a further possibility, which was that Barnes wasn't even the man's real name. If that was the case then Powell's approach had been doomed from the outset. Powell believed the man behind the desk knew the man who went by the name of Barnes and when he learned, as he undoubtedly would, about Powell's visit, the news would put Barnes on alert.

Powell decided he would try and rattle Barnes. He had nothing to lose.

"Could you please inform Mr. Barnes I stopped by?" Powell asked.

The man looked up to reply. "I'll be sure to tell him."

"And perhaps you could let him know I was hoping to catch up with him to ask about Lara." Powell didn't wait for any further acknowledgement but turned and left.

CHAPTER THIRTY ONE

Brian had given up his evening to spend it with Powell and Jenkins, studying everyone leaving the club in the hope of spotting Barnes. Powell had only the roughest description of Barnes and believed it would probably fit half the men who were members of the club but there was a small chance Brian would actually recognise Barnes as someone who worked for the Security Services.

They had been waiting an hour and were beginning to doubt the wisdom of standing outside in the cold when Powell noticed the man from behind the desk leave the club.

"Jenkins, let's follow him," Powell said on an impulse. "Brian, are you all right to stay here a bit longer?" Powell was feeling decidedly bored and following the man seemed infinitely preferable to standing doing nothing.

"Loving every minute of it," Brian answered sarcastically.

"I'll be in touch soon to let you know what we're doing," Powell promised.

Powell and Jenkins followed the man at a brisk pace for ten minutes in the direction of Soho, until he ducked inside a pub. It looked a place for locals rather than the tourists. Perhaps it was where he stopped off every night on the way home.

"I can't go in," Powell said. "He'd recognise me. I think he's been in the forces in the past so see if you can get a few drinks in him and share some experiences."

"At last, a job I'm perfectly suited for."

"Try to get him to make an evening of it."

"My pleasure," Jenkins said, smiling broadly.

"I'm going to rejoin Brian. Let me know in an hour or so how it's going."

"Will do."

Powell retraced his steps and found Brian restlessly slapping his hands together to keep warm. He probably hadn't been on an outside stakeout for a great many years. Twenty years before, neither of them would have thought twice about standing all night in the cold waiting for a sight of their target. Brian had become used to a warm office. There was nowhere indoors from where they could observe people leaving the club so they had little choice but to stand on a street corner. Powell had picked up a couple of Lattes on the way back, which improved their mood for ten minutes.

"We can't spend all night standing here," Brian said, after another half an hour. "We're not exactly inconspicuous."

"Let's wait to hear how Jenkins is getting on and then we'll make a decision on what we do next."

A short time later Powell's phone rang and he was glad to see it was Jenkins calling.

"How's it going?" Powell asked.

"He's getting our third pint in and we've only been here just over an hour. I can't keep this pace up all night."

"What's the plan for the rest of the evening?"

"First, I've got to tell you his name. He's called David Drinkwater. Can you believe that and he drinks beer like a fish. Says he doesn't touch water. Anyway, David was also in the Paras so we're already best of friends. He's single and definitely planning to make a night of it. We're talking about going for a Chinese later and then he says he has a great club he wants to show me, near Holborn."

"Keep me informed where you are. Brian and I are freezing our butts off while you enjoy yourself."

"I'd better get back, I'm supposedly having a piss at the moment."

Powell ended the call and turned back to Brian. "I think this David Drinkwater can identify Barnes and Jenkins is his new best friend. Let's go get a drink and I need to make a phone call. I have half an idea."

Two hours later Powell was at Victoria station to meet Mara and Afina. He'd sent Brian home to his wife and family. Powell was very conscious he asked a great deal of his friend and he never complained or refused his help. And all he received in return was a few steaks and drinks. Powell hoped that one day he might be able to properly return the many favours. For the last year it had all been one way traffic.

"Wow you two look hot," Powell said in greeting.

"You said we were going clubbing," Mara responded with a grin. "Just following your instructions."

"Why are we here?" Afina asked with a note of suspicion. "You are supposed to be finding Lara and I can't really imagine you wanting to go clubbing."

"Cheer up, Afina," Powell encouraged. "This is going to be a fun night out. And I'm not actually going clubbing. You guys are going out with Jenkins and his new friend."

"That explains why I get a call from Mara saying you've spoken to her and we are needed urgently. Then she adds we have to dress to impress. What's going on, Powell? I don't need you setting me up on blind dates. You didn't call me because you know I would have refused to come."

"It's not like that, Afina. I needed to speak with Mara because I wanted to ask her to do something special for me. This isn't a blind date. It's a way I hope we can find Lara."

Afina's face relaxed. "I'm sorry. In that case tell me what we have to do."

"I'll explain in the taxi."

CHAPTER THIRTY TWO

Afina and Mara arrived at the bar in Soho after a five minute ride in the taxi. Powell had explained the plan and they were both very clear about their roles. Mara was more enthusiastic than Afina.

Afina led the way into the crowded cocktail bar and spotted Jenkins sitting with a stranger. Afina and Mara walked over to the table.

Jenkins handled the introductions. "This is my girlfriend Afina and her best friend Mara. Girls, this is my new friend David."

"You lucky bastard Jenks. How did you ever get such a beautiful, young girlfriend?"

"Obviously my good looks," Jenkins joked.

"Sorry mate, I don't want to ruin our friendship before it's started but what good looks? How did you two meet?"

"I'll tell you later. I think it's your turn to buy some drinks." Jenkins realised he was going to have to agree a story with Afina about how they met.

"What would you like to drink, girls?" David asked.

"Sex on the beach," Mara answered with a mischievous smile.

"Bit pebbly in Brighton isn't it?"

"Not for me. I like being on top."

"I already like you, Mara."

"Of course you do."

"I'll have a Margherita, please," Afina interjected. Then added with a smile, "Before you forget I'm here."

"Sorry, I'll be right back with the drinks."

David went to the bar and Mara sat next to where David had been sitting on the leather seating, which ran all down one side of the bar. Afina took the vacant chair next to Jenkins.

"You okay Mara with everything?" Jenkins asked, once David was out of earshot.

"Absolutely. He looks quite cute."

"He's okay," Jenkins confirmed. "Just a bit lonely and he couldn't believe

I could get my girlfriend to meet up with us and bring a hot friend."

"I haven't had anyone call me a girlfriend for a very long time," Afina laughed. "It sounds strange."

"We're going for a meal after this drink and then he'll probably suggest a club. We're both pretty pissed already so I'm going to watch what I drink for the rest of the evening but Mara, keep his glass filled up."

"No problem."

"Afina, when he gets back I'm going to explain how we met through a mutual friend in Brighton, who owns the bar where you work. He fixed us up on a blind date."

"How long have we been together?"

"Just over a year."

"And are we planning to get married soon and have babies?"

"What…?"

"Only joking." Afina burst out laughing. Then added in a serious voice, "We haven't even had sex yet."

Mara laughed out loud. "Jenkins, you should see your face."

"Very funny," Jenkins smiled. "You make a right pair. Did Powell explain how we want the evening to end?"

"Just that we should try to end up back wherever he lives," Afina answered.

"Are we going to be having a party back at his place?" Mara asked.

"Not the sort of party you're thinking about," Afina replied, just as David returned with the drinks.

"What was that about a party?" David asked.

"I was just saying I hoped we were going to party later," Mara answered.

"That sounds an amazing idea, Mara." David's eyes looked as if they would pop out of his head at the idea. "First though we need to get a Chinese and there was a club I was going to take Jenks to but it's not really suitable for girls."

"You make your club sound interesting," Mara said. "Is it a lap dancing club by any chance?"

"Actually it is and the best in London. None of this can't touch nonsense."

"Sounds perfect to me," Mara said. "I like girls almost as much I like men."

David almost choked on his beer.

"Perhaps we will go there then after all. As long as you don't mind, Afina?"

"I don't mind," Afina replied. "I've never been to a lap dancing club though I've heard much about them. It should be fun."

"Jenks, pinch me will you please. I think I drank too much in the pub, fell asleep and this is all just a dream."

CHAPTER THIRTY THREE

The taxi dropped them off at David's apartment in Dulwich. It was three in the morning and it had been quite a night.

"I've got some booze inside," a worse for wear David said, as he stumbled from the taxi.

Mara helped support David while Jenkins paid the taxi fare.

"What a great night," Mara said to David. "And it hasn't finished yet."

David fumbled for his keys and eventually managed to insert them in the front door of the large three storey, Victorian house. He half tripped as he led the way inside and Mara had to hold on tight to his arm.

"We mustn't wake the neighbours," David cautioned, putting his finger to his lips. "I'm on the second floor."

There was a small lift, which they all squeezed inside. Once inside the apartment, David headed straight for the kitchen to find some drinks, while the others remained in the living room.

Despite the outside of the house being old, the inside of David's apartment was very bright and modern. There was a white book case along one wall and two white, leather sofas either side of a fashionable coffee table. A very large television sat in the corner of the room. A picture of David in his uniform hung above the fireplace.

"I can't drink anymore," Afina said.

"Me neither," Jenkins agreed. "We need to get David to bed, otherwise he'll be no use to us in the morning."

"I think that's my job," Mara smiled.

David came back in the room carrying a bottle of wine and some glasses.

"You have a great place," Mara said.

"Thanks. I like living here."

Mara took one of the glasses and David filled it with wine.

"Jenks, there's a beer in the fridge, if you prefer," David offered.

"Thanks but Afina and I are ready to crash, mate," Jenkins replied.

"Don't spoil the party," David urged. "Afina have some wine." He held out a glass.

Mara approached David, stood on tip toes and kissed him passionately on the lips.

"We can carry on the party by ourselves," Mara offered, stepping back. "Why don't we take the wine to your bedroom?"

"Sounds good to me," David agreed, his face lighting up at the thought. "Will you guys be all right with the sofas?"

"We're good, thanks," Jenkins answered.

"I'll get you some blankets."

David led Mara to his bedroom and shortly after returned with a couple of sleeping bags.

"Afina, does Mara have a boyfriend?" David asked.

"No. Why do you ask?"

"I really like her. I was just wondering if this is a one off or maybe we'll be able to see each other again."

Afina felt a pang of guilt as she answered, "Well, she doesn't have a boyfriend."

David headed for his bedroom with a large smile on his face.

"Are you sure Mara doesn't mind doing this?" Jenkins asked.

"Did she look like she minded?"

"I guess not."

"She's an escort. She sleeps with strangers every day. David seems really nice and knowing Mara, I'm sure she will actually have fun. He certainly will."

"I'm feeling a bit jealous."

"Do you fancy Mara?"

"That wasn't what I meant."

"So what did you mean?"

"Nothing really. Just the booze always makes me feel a bit horny and..."

"And you're stuck here with me instead of in bed with Mara."

"No it's not that. Well, it's sort of that. It would be easier if you weren't here. You're beautiful and you're off limits."

"What do you mean, I'm off limits?"

"Well you know... you and Powell."

"What about me and Powell?"

"Bloody hell, Afina. You know full well what I mean. You and Powell have a special relationship. You're meant for each other. I couldn't come between you two. Not that I think for a second you'd be interested in me anyway."

"Powell loves me like a daughter. We aren't ever going to have a proper relationship."

"Don't worry, he'll see sense eventually. I've seen the way he looks at you. It isn't the way someone looks at their daughter."

"Maybe," Afina said doubtfully. "But perhaps I don't want to be with Powell. And why do you say, I'd never be interested in you? I happen to think you're one of the nicest men I know."

"That proves it!" Jenkins exclaimed.

"I don't understand."

"You just called me nice. That means you would never sleep with me."

"No it doesn't."

"So you would like to sleep with me?"

"Well…"

Jenkins laughed. "Don't answer, Afina. I'm teasing you. Just getting my own back."

"That's not fair. I'm feeling quite tipsy."

"Listen, you should try and get some sleep. At least we have a sofa each. We're going to be up early."

"I'm not looking forward to the morning."

"David is a decent guy. When we explain everything to him, he'll be okay," Jenkins promised, although he was far from certain how David would react.

"I hope so."

There was the sound of giggling coming from the nearby bedroom.

"I hope there not going to be too noisy," Jenkins said.

"This is Mara we're talking about. I don't think she does quietly."

"I'm going to text Powell to let him know everything is ready for the morning."

Afina took off her jeans and Jenkins couldn't help but glance at her. She had long slim legs. Then she climbed inside the sleeping bag and lay down on the sofa.

Jenkins sent the text message and then turned off the light. He wrapped his sleeping bag around himself and lay down on his sofa. He'd had many far worse beds for the night when in the army.

A few minutes after getting comfortable there were the unmistakeable sounds of two people having sex, coming from the bedroom.

Jenkins could hear Afina tossing and turning, struggling to get comfortable.

"Noisy buggers aren't they," Jenkins commented after a minute.

"Makes falling asleep difficult," Afina laughed.

Afina hadn't had sex for a very long time and listening to Mara and David was making her excited. Her hand fell between her legs and she could feel her moisture. She stroked herself a couple of times and inserted one finger. This is absurd. I can't masturbate with Jenkins just a few feet away.

"I'm going to get a beer," Jenkins announced. "Do you want anything?"

"I'll have one as well, please. I'm not going to be able to sleep until they've finished."

Afina sat up on the sofa and moved her hand away from between her legs.

Jenkins handed her a can of beer and sat back on his sofa.

"I wonder where Lara is right now?" Afina asked. "I hope she's all right."

"Wherever she is, she knows Powell will be doing everything possible to find her. That should give her strength."

"Powell's lucky to have you as a friend."

"He's a good man. One of the best I've come across."

CHAPTER THIRTY FOUR

Jenkins checked his watch. It was six thirty. He was feeling very tired but not too hungover as he'd drunk very little in the latter part of the evening. He quietly opened the door to the apartment and then went downstairs and opened the door to the house. Powell was waiting outside and followed him back upstairs and into David's living room. Afina was still asleep on the sofa.

"We only got to sleep about four this morning," Jenkins explained.

"How's Drinkwater?"

"I don't think Mara let him have much sleep and he's going to have a massive hangover."

"Let's make some coffee and then wake him up," Powell suggested.

"He isn't going to be happy. He doesn't start work until ten so was planning on getting up at nine."

"We can't wait that long."

"He isn't going to be happy when he sees you."

Powell shrugged his shoulders. "Let's hope he is the decent guy you say he is."

Jenkins went into the small kitchen and found tea bags but no real coffee, only instant. He decided to make tea for everyone and was just finishing when Afina appeared.

"Can I help?" she asked.

"Thanks, you can carry a couple of cups in for me."

Back in the living room they placed the cups on the coffee table.

"Time to get them up," Powell said. "Jenkins, I think you should have the pleasure. Wake Mara first if you can and send her out here. Then wake your new friend and tell him you want to speak to him in the living room. Remind him about work if he's reluctant to get up."

"I get all the best jobs," Jenkins smiled.

A short time later Mara joined them in the living room.

"Fuck, that was some night," Mara said, rubbing her eyes.

"So we heard," Afina answered.

"Actually, I was referring to the night out, not the sex. Though that wasn't bad either to be fair. He's a nice guy. I don't know how he's going to react to this."

A full ten minutes went by and Powell was beginning to wonder if Jenkins was having a problem, when finally he emerged from the bedroom.

"I've told him roughly what's going on but not the details," Jenkins informed everyone. "He wasn't going to get out of bed otherwise."

"How did he take it?"

"Quite well all things considered. Called me a few names at first but I asked him if he'd had a good night and he said it was the best in a very long time. I said we all like him and need his help so he's getting dressed and will be out in a minute."

David entered the room with hair at all angles and very bloodshot eyes. Afina offered him a cup of tea, which he accepted. He sat on the sofa and looked up expectantly.

"I told Jenks I'd give you five minutes."

Powell stepped nearer to the chair and David seemed to register his presence for the first time.

"You're the fuckwit pretended he wanted to join the club yesterday," David said. "Suppose I shouldn't be surprised. So you're Jenks friend he mentioned needs my help."

"I am. Sorry about the deceit but we're getting desperate. A friend of ours was kidnapped yesterday morning and her life is in severe danger. We're just hoping she isn't already dead."

"I'm sorry to hear that but what do you want from me?"

"You know what I want. I need you to identify Barnes for me because he's responsible for the kidnapping."

"Do you know why I'm employed by the club?" It was a rhetorical question. "Because I'm ex-army and half the members work for some part of the government. They trust me to keep their secrets. So why should I believe anything you tell me. For all I know you work for some foreign government and are trying to trap Barnes in some way."

"I run a bar in Brighton," Powell answered. "You know Jenkins is truly from your old regiment. Afina is the manager of my bar and Mara really is her best friend."

"I don't trust a word you say. You've all been lying to me since the first moment I met you."

"The only lie we've told you is my pretending Afina is my girlfriend," Jenkins responded. "I'm not actually that lucky."

"And I wasn't lying when I said I liked you," Mara added. "I think I demonstrated how much I like you."

David smiled. "That's very true."

"How about, after we've finished talking, I demonstrate again how much I like you? If you've got the energy?"

"Sounds good to me."

Powell had to smile. He doubted he any longer had David's full attention as he would be thinking about Mara and what was to come later. At least he hadn't kicked them out of the apartment.

"Okay, I'm going to tell you everything we know," Powell said. "And then you can decide whether to help us or not."

CHAPTER THIRTY FIVE

David had listened to their story and agreed to help. Powell believed Mara was the deciding factor in his decision. David had fallen for her big time and was hopeful of seeing her again, something Mara had encouraged. Powell wasn't sure how he would react if he ever discovered what she did for a living.

David informed Powell that he doubted Barnes was the man's real name but he didn't actually know his real name. Many of the members used pseudonyms and he believed Barnes was one of those because on a couple of occasions, David had addressed him as Mr Barnes and he had been slow to respond, a clear indication it wasn't his real name.

Powell was concerned they could do nothing but wait for Barnes to appear at the club, when they would receive a call from David. Fortunately, David said Barnes ate lunch most days at the club and also often dropped by in the evening for drinks.

Powell wasn't sure if Lara was still alive but she had been in their hands for twenty four hours and he had to assume they wouldn't be planning to keep her alive for very much longer. If their objective in kidnapping her was to discover what she knew, then he doubted she would hold out for very long under the type of interrogation she had described Al-Hashimi receiving and once she told them everything, she would have served her purpose and be killed. Time was therefore of the essence but frustratingly, nothing could progress until Barnes arrived at the club.

Afina and Mara had returned to Brighton leaving Powell and Jenkins to enjoy a large cooked breakfast in a café not far from the club. Powell had updated Brian on events but asked him not to share anything with anyone within work. No one could be trusted and until Lara was safe, he didn't want anyone being forewarned about their plans.

The call from David came at just after midday and it took Powell and Jenkins only five minutes to walk to the club. Powell had decided he would try and meet with Barnes alone so Jenkins stayed outside as Powell entered the club. David was behind his desk and immediately picked up an internal phone. A minute later a man arrived and took over his position at the desk.

"I'll show you to the meeting room," David explained. "Then I will tell Barnes you are here to see him. As agreed, I will tell him your name is Brown. Hopefully that will pique his curiosity sufficiently for him to want to meet with you."

"Let's hope it all goes smoothly," Powell answered, following David to a small meeting room with panelled wood and impressive portraits hanging on the walls, most of which were more than a hundred years old.

Powell sat facing the door so he could be prepared for whoever entered. When the door opened after a few minutes, Powell quickly decided the man posed no physical threat and was most likely the man calling himself Barnes. He certainly fitted the description provided by Brown.

Barnes appraised Powell before demanding, "Who are you?"

"My name is Powell."

"I've heard of you. Your the man who runs the bar in Brighton."

"Correct but I'm at a disadvantage, I don't know your name."

"Barnes will do fine," he replied with a small smile. "What do you want Powell? Why are you here?"

Powell was surprised Barnes was maintaining such a cool exterior. He didn't seem unduly concerned by Powell's sudden arrival.

"I want Lara back," Powell stated firmly. "And she better not be harmed."

"I don't really think you're in any position to threaten me."

"Really? I think you should be very worried. It won't be difficult for me to find out who you are and then I have only to speak with my contacts at MI5 and I'm sure they will want to understand why you never passed on the name Al-Hashimi. And that will only be the start of your troubles because there will be a great deal of explaining to do about your American friends."

"I think, Powell, you have put two and two together and made five. The best thing you can do is go back to Brighton and your bar. Lara has been arrested under ant-terrorism laws for helping terrorists in Saudi Arabia. I don't know what rubbish she told you but she is a threat to this country's security."

"Don't give me that shit. You're acting illegally."

"I assure you, everything I do is perfectly legal and in the interests of this country."

"So where is Lara being held?"

"We're not in the habit of telling just anyone where we are holding a terrorist suspect. Go back to Brighton and forget about Lara. Otherwise, we might see the need to investigate you further."

"I will go back to Brighton and develop amnesia if you tell me where to find Lara. Otherwise, I'm going to make your life hell. I don't care what games you're playing but I do care about my friend. If you harm Lara, I promise you will live to regret it."

"Don't threaten me. I'm not some junior flunky. I'm warning you to keep your nose out of my affairs or else…"

"Or else what?" Powell asked, as he grabbed Barnes by the lapels of his suit and pinned him back against the wall. At the same time he stuck the small listening device under one lapel. Once again he was grateful to Brian for his help.

After a moment, Powell stepped back and smoothed down the jacket lapels. "Let's stop threatening each other. What do I have to do or say to convince you to return Lara?"

"You don't have anything I want," Barnes snapped.

Powell's initial pleasure at finally being face to face with Barnes was diminishing rapidly. He had thought Barnes would wilt under the pressure of his very presence but he had badly miscalculated. If it was pure bravado, Barnes was doing it well. There was little more Powell could achieve through threats.

"I'm sorry you don't want to cooperate," Powell said evenly. "I came here to try and broker a deal. My silence for the safe return of Lara. I can see I am probably wasting my time but I will give you two hours to think about what I've said. If I don't hear from Lara within the next two hours, I will make more noise than you ever thought possible. I take this personally and I am holding you responsible for my friend's welfare. If anything happens to her, I swear you will see me again and next time, I won't be so polite."

"I don't expect to see you again," Barnes replied. "I suggest you leave before I have security throw you out."

Powell stood up and walked to the door without looking back.

CHAPTER THIRTY SIX

Powell stopped by David's desk on the way out.

"Did you get what you want?" David asked.

"Not really but at least I now know what he looks like. Are there any other exits from here?"

"Yes, there's one at the rear."

"Thanks for your help. Sorry again about last night. I didn't think you'd help if we just approached you normally."

"You're right. I'd have told you to fuck off. Mara is rather more persuasive."

Powell smiled. "I'm sure she is."

"Listen, Powell, if I can help further let me know. I hope you find your friend."

"Thanks."

"Perhaps we can all go for a drink again when this is all over?"

"Just give her a call and ask her out."

"What do you mean?"

"Mara. Just call her. Don't wait for us all to get together again just so you can see her."

"I'm not sure I'm her type of bloke. She's a very special girl."

"How does that motto go? He who dares wins."

David smiled. "I suppose you're right."

"I need to get going. Remember, I own a very nice bar in Brighton so anytime you want a few beers come and see me. The drinks will be on me. You've been a great help. And if you let me know you're coming I'll get Afina to invite Mara over."

"That would be brilliant," David replied with a huge grin.

Powell shook hands and left. He decided he liked David Drinkwater.

On the street, Powell briefly told Jenkins about his meeting with Barnes. "He's a pretty cool character but hopefully I've ruffled a few feathers. How is reception?"

"Loud and clear. Immediately after you left, he made a phone call and arranged to urgently meet someone at his home. Said the club was no longer safe to meet."

"What was this person's name?"

"Neither of them used names on the phone.

"We need to stay close to him and find out who he is meeting. There's a rear exit he might use so we need to be alert."

"I can track him from my phone. Brian has some really neat toys. I've not come across a dual purpose bug like that before, which transmits voice and location."

"Let's grab a taxi," Powell said, stepping in to the road with his hand in the air.

A black cab quickly cut across another car, receiving a blast from the driver's horn, and pulled to a stop at the pavement. They both climbed in the back.

"Where we going?" the cab driver asked.

Powell reached forward and handed a twenty pound note through the hole in the glass partition. "We're still deciding. That's just a tip."

"Fine with me," the driver replied. "Let me know when you've decided."

Jenkins was studying his phone. "He's on the move. Must have used the rear entrance. Driver, we need to head for Grosvenor Square."

The driver pulled out into the traffic.

"Turn down Park Lane," Jenkins directed.

Powell said nothing as they tracked what was presumably another taxi up ahead, along the Cromwell Road towards Hammersmith. Jenkins continued to give directions as they crossed Hammersmith Bridge. A couple of miles further and Powell noticed the road sign.

"Do you see where we are?" Powell asked.

Jenkins looked up. "We're in Hammersmith, aren't we?"

"No, we just left Hammersmith. We're now in Barnes."

"Barnes. Didn't know there was such a place. Interesting coincidence." He looked back down at his phone. "Looks like we've arrived."

Powell could see the taxi up ahead at the side of the street. Barnes was paying the driver through the car window. He glanced around and then went inside the house.

Powell paid the thirty pound fare and added another ten pound tip. They were in a very expensive residential street and even though the houses were in semidetached pairs, Powell knew the houses would cost millions.

"We can't stand around out here," Powell said. "His visitor might arrive any minute. Let's go check out those shops and see if we can get a coffee."

They found two coffee shops and chose the nearest to the house. Jenkins was listening to Barnes through headphones but to the casual observer just looked like he was listening to music.

Powell sent Brian a text with the address where the man calling himself Barnes lived and asked him to check who actually lived there. Before he received a response another taxi drew up in front of the house. A man in his fifties stepped out and walked quickly up the path to the front door.

CHAPTER THIRTY SEVEN

As Barnes opened the door to his visitor, Jenkins was trying to unobtrusively take pictures of them both on his phone.

"What's so bloody important, I have to come all the way out here?" Crawford asked impatiently, once inside the house. "I can't always just drop everything I'm doing and come running like this, I'm a busy man."

"Do you want a drink?" Barnes asked pleasantly, ignoring the outburst. He found Crawford prone to loud and unnecessary outbursts. He lacked manners.

"I don't drink during the day." Crawford made it sound like a crime worthy of capital punishment.

Barnes had already helped himself to a whisky. He didn't care what the damned American thought.

"I can make you tea," Barnes offered. He knew full well Crawford didn't like tea. "Or would you like some water, perhaps?"

"What I'd like, is to know why the club is no longer safe to meet?"

"I had a visit from that Powell chap this morning. Bloody cheek of him. He just wandered in the club pretending his name was Brown and threatened me. He said if he didn't hear from the Lara woman within two hours, he was going to cause a stink."

Crawford was thoughtful for a moment. "So he knows who you are?"

"I doubt if he knows my real name. He must have found me through your man Brown. I told you he wasn't up to the job. He must have told Powell about our meeting at the club."

"We need to get rid of Powell. Set up a meet."

"On what pretext? He just wants to get the damned woman back."

"Tell Powell, I need to meet with him to be confident he's going to keep his end of the bargain and keep his mouth shut. Tell him we'll bring Lara to the meeting. And he's to come alone."

"He's no fool. He might smell a trap."

"If he wants to see Lara alive, tell him he has no choice. If he continues with his threats we will be forced to get rid of her. He seems to care for her so I'm sure he will agree to a meeting. We need to choose a place that makes him feel safe."

"Do you have somewhere in mind?" Barnes asked.

"It needs to be somewhere busy and central. I have an idea and we might be able to kill two birds with one stone."

"Are you going to go?" Jenkins asked.

"I think I have to. The good news is the confirmation Lara is still alive. They don't know we are expecting trouble and I'll have you with me as backup."

They had listened to the entire conversation from within the house while sat drinking coffee.

"But they are going to try and kill you and Lara. At least I assume that's what he meant by killing two birds with one stone. If it's somewhere crowded you won't even see them coming."

"Then you better do a good job of watching my back."

"And what if there are several of them?"

"They won't try anything while I'm with Barnes and the American. We just have to keep our eyes peeled for danger."

Jenkins didn't look convinced. "Okay. Let's wait and see where they suggest meeting."

They saw the front door open and the visitor leave. "Try and get a photo of him," Powell urged.

Jenkins sprang to his feet and headed outside. Powell watched him walk a little way down the road but with his back to him, couldn't be sure what success he was having with taking photos.

The visitor waved down a taxi and Jenkins returned to the cafe.

"Did you get some?" Powell asked.

Jenkins regained his seat and looked at his phone for a minute, checking the photos. He handed the phone to an impatient Powell.

"Good photos of his back," Powell acknowledged.

"Sorry."

"It can't be helped. At least the photos of Barnes are clear enough to get an identification. I'll send a copy to Brian."

Powell's phone rang. It was a withheld number.

"Powell," he answered.

"My colleague wants to meet with you," Barnes said. "He is willing to return the woman, if he is convinced you can both be trusted to keep your mouth shut. He plans to spell out to you why it would be foolish not to keep quiet."

"When and where?" Powell answered without hesitation.

"We thought you'd feel safer somewhere busy so Leicester Square. There's a Mexican restaurant next to the Odeon cinema. We'll be there at six."

"Sounds good to me. Make sure you bring Lara. And no funny business."

"Lara will definitely be there."

"Good. Then life can go back to normal for all of us. I can run my bar and you can get back to whatever it is you do."

CHAPTER THIRTY EIGHT

Powell and Jenkins went straight from Barnes to Leicester Square. It was still four hours until the meeting but Powell wanted to check out the restaurant and the general area outside.

They walked slowly around Leicester Square and as usual the place was swamped with people, a large number of them tourists. There were numerous potential targets for terrorists and in the crowds it would also be easy for someone to make an attempt on his life, walking to or from the restaurant.

Powell was old enough to remember the assassination of Georgi Markov on a London street via a micro-engineered pellet containing ricin, fired into his leg via an umbrella wielded by someone associated with the Bulgarian secret police or KGB. Markov thought he had suffered an insect bite but that evening he became ill and there being no antidote for ricin, four days later he was dead. It was one of the scenarios discussed in his training when he joined MI5.

The restaurant had a small front entrance on the Square but once inside was large and went back a long way. They sat at a table near the entrance and ordered some tapas and a couple of pints of San Miguel. Powell wasn't really hungry but he wanted to become familiar with the interior before the meeting.

He went to the toilet and used the opportunity to check for other exits. He wasn't surprised to find an emergency exit at the rear. Back in his seat, he wondered if the opposition already had men in place. He glanced around the restaurant but there were no obvious candidates.

Powell's phone rang and he was pleased to see it was Brian.

"What do you know?" Powell asked.

"Nothing, which is very scary."

"What do you mean?"

"We ran the photo through our facial recognition software and there was no hit. There is also no one living at the address in Barnes. "

"I don't understand." Powell had been certain he had collected enough information to make identifying Barnes an easy task.

"Neither do I. If he worked for any branch of the government we should have had a match."

"So who does he work for?"

"Almost certainly MI6…"

"But you just said…"

"I said we should have had a match. The fact we didn't is scary because it means he probably works for a small clandestine element of MI6, which doesn't officially even exist. They have virtually unlimited power and their directive is simply to do whatever it takes to combat terrorism. They sit outside the normal structures of MI6 and report directly to the Home Secretary."

"Are you sure they exist? I mean, it's not just one of those urban myths MI5 likes to attribute to MI6?"

"Nobody will admit to their existence but I've suspected there is such a group for some time. If he works for them, it helps explain the American connection. They were supposedly born out of nine eleven to work with the Americans. It was felt there was a new era of terrorism and it needed a new unit to combat it."

"Brian, whoever these people are, we know they have not been sanctioned to commit kidnapping and murder in the UK. Unlike the Americans, we don't hold people for years without trial."

"That may be the whole point."

"What do you mean?"

"In the UK if we arrest someone then indeed they end up in court. If you don't think you are going to like what they say in court, then you need to keep them outside of the justice system. The extreme interpretation of that is to have them killed rather than formally arrested."

"But that is never legal."

"I'm not sure. It depends on the remit of the people pulling the trigger. It wasn't so different in your day. Things were done in the name of fighting terrorism that were illegal according to the laws of the time."

"All I know is that they can't go around killing members of the public because of some perceived rather than actual risk. Lara and I are happy to keep our mouths shut but it seems they still want us dead."

"I didn't say it was right just the reality."

"By the way," Powell said, changing subject. "I think we've lost contact with Barnes. I don't know whether he just changed his clothes or found the bug but we've picked up zero sound and it's saying he hasn't moved from the house for the last two hours."

"Could be taking a sleep."

"Not very likely given everything that's happening."

"Pity, would have been nice to know what they were saying leading up to the meeting."

"Actually, thinking about it, he probably just changed his jacket. If he'd found it, he would have used it to feed us false information."

"True," Brian agreed. "I need to get going and see if I can uncover more about Barnes. I'll see you later."

CHAPTER THIRTY NINE

As six o'clock approached, Powell was getting nervous. Brian's revelation about Barnes possible role within MI6 was extremely worrying. He had described a group of people working outside the law, able to command significant resources and ruthless in their intent.

Powell had reached the conclusion it would be a minor miracle if they were all to make it back to Brighton in one piece. He was pleased Afina was out of harm's way. Lara, Brian and he had all made career decisions, which at least in part, had led to them being in this situation. Jenkins was a former soldier turned mercenary so had definitely chosen a dangerous lifestyle. Afina had made no such choices but encountered an enormous amount of danger over the last year. At least on this occasion she was one less person for him to worry about.

Jenkins and Brian were sat inside the restaurant, several tables away from where Powell had chosen to sit for his second visit of the day. He had decided he would arrive early and choose where they sat. He selected a table for four and told the waitress his friends would be arriving shortly. He occupied a seat facing the entrance, ordered another pint of San Miguel and awaited their arrival.

At five minutes past six Barnes and the American entered the restaurant. Powell caught their attention and they strode to his table. No handshakes were offered as the two men sat down opposite Powell.

A waitress immediately appeared. "Can I get you a drink," she asked.

"Gin and tonic," Barnes answered.

"Just fizzy water for me," Crawford requested.

"Where's Lara?" Powell asked. His plan was to leave with Lara by the rear exit but that required Lara's presence in the restaurant.

"Close by," Crawford answered. "So you're the man been causing all this trouble?"

"I don't want to cause any trouble. I just want to take my friend back to Brighton and forget any of this ever happened."

"I looked you up," Crawford continued. "Seems you've got a habit of poking your nose in where it isn't wanted. And you're daughter was much the same."

Powell gripped tightly to the edge of the table. He was close to pulling the American from his seat and beating him to a pulp.

"Say one more thing about my daughter," Powell warned. "And you won't be able to walk out of this restaurant. She was a police officer doing her duty. Doing it better than you two I suspect."

"Don't be touchy. We all serve in different ways," Crawford responded.

The waitress returned with their drinks, which gave Powell a chance to compose himself. He concluded that as the American was doing all the talking, he must be the senior partner in the relationship with Barnes.

"So when do I get to see Lara?" Powell asked, once the waitress had left.

"Shortly," Crawford responded. "First, I want to make something very clear. If, after tonight, you or the woman do anything to put at risk my work, you will both be removed."

"I love the way you use euphemisms to describe murder. That is what it would be and in our country it is still illegal, last I checked."

"War is not illegal if it's sanctioned by the government," Barnes spoke for the first time.

"No one has declared war," Powell replied.

"The terrorists declared war when they hijacked the planes and flew them into the towers," Crawford said. "They asked for a war and we're giving it to them."

"I think you're missing the point," Powell said. "Lara was also fighting terrorism and I certainly haven't done anything to support it, yet you sent men to kill us. I don't see how that is part of your so called war against terror."

"Don't be naïve. Sometimes there's a bigger picture. In this case a massively bigger one..." Crawford started to explain.

"I don't give a dam about your bigger picture," Powell interrupted angrily. "I just want to take Lara home. You go play your games somewhere else."

Crawford sat back in his chair. "I can see we aren't going to agree but I think it is safe to let Lara go. I suspect you have feelings for her that go beyond normal friendship. And I'm not surprised, she's a fine looking woman."

The waitress appeared again. "Are you ready to order food?" she asked.

"Come back in five minutes," Crawford replied dismissively.

"Lara is at best a friend," Powell stated. "And to be honest, it's a stretch to even call her that. I'd help anyone in her predicament. Unlike you two, I believe in the rule of law."

"Very noble sentiments," Crawford said scornfully. "I've heard enough sanctimonious twaddle. Go stand outside the restaurant. My men are holding Lara on the other side of the Square. They'll send her over to you when they see you. Then go get on the next train back to Brighton."

"Aren't you coming?" Powell asked.

"We have other things to discuss," Crawford replied. "So we'll stay and order some food."

Powell stood up with a degree of uncertainty. He suspected the moment he left the restaurant, he would become the target for Crawford's men but he had little choice. He had to check to see if Lara was outside.

"I warn you," Powell threatened. "If you're playing games and I'm walking into some sort of trap outside, you better be sure they finish the job because otherwise I'm going to come back in here and kill you both."

"Don't be paranoid," Crawford replied. "She's out there. Just remember to keep your mouth shut once you return to Brighton. You won't get a second chance."

A young couple were just about to leave the restaurant and he sped up so that he followed them through the door. He felt a little guilty he was using them as a human shield. He hoped he had managed to block the view of anyone intending him harm but once out on the pavement, he quickly ducked to the side, crouched low to tie his shoe lace and at the same time tried to spot danger.

There was a white van parked on the south side of the Square with its door open. A couple of men stood in front of the van peering in his direction. Powell finished with his shoe lace and stood back up. He looked straight at the two men and they immediately recognised him and reacted by turning back towards the open van door.

Powell saw the men pull Lara from within the van and hold her under each arm. She looked weak and they seemed to be supporting her body not just keeping her from running away. Powell had realised there was every possibility she had been hurt, possibly seriously, by interrogation. At a distance of fifty metres he thought she looked unsteady on her legs and he could detect bruising on her face.

He started to walk slowly towards Lara and the men hurriedly jumped back inside the van and drove away. Powell was surprised that Lara seemed disorientated and uncertain what to do. She stood on the pavement looking around until she spotted him walking in her direction. There was no sign of a smile or urgency to walk towards him. Powell wondered if she had been given drugs to make her compliant.

CHAPTER FORTY

Lara was in a daze. She realised she was outside for the first time in what seemed a long time but she didn't understand where she was or why. She didn't recognise her surroundings but she was happy to see the men who had been holding her prisoner, drive away in the van. She felt unsteady on her feet and hungover but she hadn't been drinking. She was decidedly disorientated.

She looked to her right and saw a cinema. There was another cinema off to the left across the green. It was the Odeon and seemed vaguely familiar. She felt sure she had been there to watch films. She took a couple of tentative steps forward but she was having to force one foot in front of the other. She felt weighed down and every step was hard work.

Her brain wasn't functioning properly. Then she remembered the men holding her down and inserting a needle in her arm. The next thing she knew she was being pulled out of the van. She must have been drugged.

She looked ahead and could see someone she recognised. It was Powell walking towards her. She took a couple of steps in his direction but it was ridiculously hard work. Her head was clearing a little but her breathing was laboured.

Suddenly she realised why she was having trouble breathing. There was something tight around her body. She felt like she was wrapped in cling film. She pulled down the zip on the jacket she was wearing. The shock of what she saw made her freeze on the spot. She had no doubt it was a bomb fitted tightly like a vest over her shoulders and around her middle. She shook her head trying to be sure she was awake. Surely she must be dreaming?

She pinched herself on the arm and for the first time knew with absolute certainty she was very much awake and a walking bomb. She was surrounded with people and if the bomb was to detonate there would be massive casualties.

Her first instinct was to tear the vest from her body but she suspected if she touched anything it would immediately detonate. She had no expertise in disarming bombs. She needed help urgently.

Powell was coming closer. She needed help but she didn't want him to get close. She didn't want anyone to get close. To her left the grass Square had only a few people walking through, rather than the large crowds thronging the pavements. The weather was cool enough to ensure people didn't stop to sit on the benches.

She instinctively knew what she had to do. She ran through the small metal gate in to the central square, shouting that she had a bomb and holding open her jacket. People were slow to react at first but then noticed the evidence of a bomb around her body and started screaming and running away in all directions.

She was terrified yet calm. Her senses seemed heightened. She felt the cold breath of the wind on her cheek. She heard the screams of the young child being unceremoniously dragged away by its mother above the louder screams of the many adults.

She felt a deep sadness that her life was unfulfilled. She would never experience motherhood and so many other things. How would her father cope with the news? Certainly not well. She looked to the sky and then back to Powell. He was a good man. He was a strong man and she knew he would find those responsible.

Powell didn't understand why Lara had ignored him and ran on to the grass square. She had definitely recognised him. Then he heard the screams of terror and saw the people running away from Lara.

He started running towards her, not quite understanding what was happening but knowing she needed help. At the gate he was forced to come to a stop by the number of people running through the gate in the opposite direction, all seemingly desperate to get away from Lara.

He looked at Lara and she was nodding her head vigorously from side to side and shouting at him to stay away. She was pointing at her body and he realised at last why everyone was terrified and running away. He could see the suicide vest under her coat.

An instinct made Powell look back towards the restaurant and he saw the American standing at the entrance looking in his direction. He had a phone to his ear and everything became crystal clear.

The entrance to the square was now free. He wanted to go to Lara but realised that would be signing her death warrant. The American was waiting for the moment when they were close together so he could kill them both. He had only to hit the connect button on his phone and the bomb would detonate.

Powell took a few steps backwards and looked again towards the American. He nodded his head, begging him not to go ahead. He looked back at Lara and saw her lie herself down on the ground. She was a brave woman and doing everything possible to minimise casualties. There was chaos but Lara's running to the centre of the square had undoubtedly saved many lives.

Powell felt helpless. He felt a desperate sadness for Lara's plight and also a burning anger towards the American. He was still trying to decide what to do when the decision was taken out of his hands. Lara exploded with a deafening noise and he was knocked backwards onto the ground.

CHAPTER FORTY ONE

Powell awoke to find himself staring at a plain white ceiling. He turned his head slowly to the side and received proof he was in a hospital room as he'd first suspected.

"How are you feeling?" Jenkins asked, sat in a chair at the side of the bed.

"Head hurts like hell."

"You cracked it on the pavement when you were thrown back by the blast. It was lucky you didn't get any closer."

"I can't believe those bastards just blew her up like that."

"What happened exactly?"

"They strapped a bomb to her and dumped her on the street. The American wanted her and me to get close and then he was going to detonate the bomb but she ruined his plans. She knew she was a walking bomb so she ran away from everyone and threw herself to the ground."

"They're saying she was a suicide bomber."

"She was a bloody hero… What was the casualty toll?"

"No fatalities," Jenkins answered. "Some broken bones. A few cuts and bruises."

"Thank God. That's thanks to Lara's quick thinking."

"What are we going to do about it?" Jenkins asked. "Lara wasn't my favourite woman but we can't stand by and let them get away with this."

"I agree but we need to tread carefully. They were willing to kill an enormous number of people just to get at me and Lara. They will obviously stop at nothing. I don't want anyone else getting killed because of me."

"Don't go blaming yourself for Lara's death. It wasn't your fault."

"I know but if I don't back off and someone else gets killed, it will be my fault."

"So who is responsible for Lara's death?" Jenkins asked.

"Not sure but the Americans are current favourites. The American in the restaurant was definitely in charge. Barnes was just his lapdog. And it was the American who detonated Lara's bomb."

"Brian thinks he may know the American. He's not certain but thinks he may work for the CIA or at least has done in the past. He went back to the office to check."

"It doesn't seem possible the CIA could be detonating bombs in central London. It doesn't make sense... What time is it?"

"Eight thirty." Jenkins pointed at a clock on the wall.

"So I've been out for over two hours."

"They want to keep you in here overnight. They are worried you have a concussion. Obviously don't know how hard headed you are."

"I'm not staying here. I'll discharge myself. I can't be confined to a bed. I suspect the American isn't going to give up and just let me live out my days quietly. He has too much to lose and I make an easy target in here. Talking of him, what happened after the bomb went off?"

"In the panic, the American and Barnes simply walked away. We stayed because we were worried about you."

"Thanks."

"There must be more at stake than just Lara seeing them break the rules about how a prisoner is interrogated."

"I agree. It's almost as if they want to promote terrorism," Powell suggested. Then he realised the significance of his casual observation. "That must be it. They want to increase the perceived threat from terrorism. If we're all running scared, we're more likely to agree to anything the war mongers suggest. It's a bit like telling everyone Saddam Hussain had weapons of mass destruction. It made the public happy for us to invade Iraq."

"But I don't get why they captured Al-Hashimi? If they want acts of terrorism to go ahead then surely they should have left him alone."

"Perhaps they have their own agenda. They want to control what acts of terrorism occur and where. If they had managed to kill Lara when they first tried, then they would have been able to blow up whatever or whomever they wanted and then blame Al-Hashimi for everything, when they were finished."

"You do realise what you're suggesting?" Jenkins queried. "Maybe that bang on your head was harder than we first realised."

"I know it sounds mad but do you have a better explanation?"

"Not right now. Why are the Americans involved?"

"We're turning soft as partners. After what happened in Iraq and Afghanistan, the government is running scared of getting too involved in further Middle East operations. Hell, we even have an opposition leader committed to cutting back on defence spending. That can't be making the Americans happy."

"If you're right then we could be talking about very senior people in government being involved," Jenkins surmised. "I don't like the odds."

"All the more reason to get out of this hospital asap," Powell said, pulling back his bed cover and swinging his legs over the side of the bed. He felt a little groggy but it was no worse than a hangover. "Go find a nurse and tell them I'm leaving."

CHAPTER FORTY TWO

Powell had ignored all the protestations from the doctor. Jenkins stood by smiling at the doctor's initial refusal to let him leave. He was wasting his breath. When eventually the doctor realised nothing would change Powell's mind, he had made him sign a form abdicating the hospital of all responsibility.

They were at Victoria station in time to catch the nine thirty two train to Brighton. Powell had some strong pain killers prescribed by the doctor, who had told him under no circumstances to drink or drive while taking the pills. Jenkins didn't bother reminding Powell of the doctor's instructions when they arrived at the station and Powell headed straight to buy miniature whiskies and cans of ginger ales.

"Hey, I'm adding a mixer to the whisky," Powell said, noticing the look on Jenkins face once they were sat on the train.

"And I thought you'd bought the whisky just for me," Jenkins joked. "But I'd do the same in your place. It's been that kind of day."

Powell took a large drink and then took out his phone and called Brian, who immediately revealed he did know the American. His name was Crawford and they had met at some meeting in the distant past about joint cooperation against drug trafficking. That had been in the days when the CIA was more worried about drug cartels than ISIS. Brian had looked Crawford up and he'd been easy to find. He was now a Deputy Director at the CIA.

"Deputy Director! That's seriously important," Powell reacted.

"It is," Brian agreed. "It means we have to tread carefully. He's a very powerful man."

"My brain is too fuddled to deal with this right now. Let's talk in the morning."

"I'll see what else I can find out about Crawford," Brian promised.

"Brian, can you please get me the number for Lara's father. He deserves to know the truth about his daughter."

"I'm not sure that's a good idea. If you tell him the truth, you risk putting his life in danger. He's likely to cause a stink and you don't get to Crawford's position without being ruthless. He isn't the sort of man to let anyone get in the way of his plans."

"Okay, get me the number and I'll leave it a couple of days before calling."

Powell bid Brian good night and updated Jenkins on the news about Crawford.

"I have to say, it's never boring being around you," Jenkins said.

"Sorry," Powell apologised but he was smiling.

"Hell, I meant it as a compliment."

"Has anyone let Afina know what happened tonight?" Powell asked. When he went to call Brian he'd noticed he had five missed calls.

"I told her you were in hospital and she shouldn't worry but that was hours ago."

"Sorry I didn't call earlier," he said, when Afina answered. "Jenkins and I are on a train to Brighton, gets in about ten thirty."

"So you are okay?" Afina asked, obviously relieved.

"I'm fine. I just fell over and banged my head."

"It took you long enough to let me know. I'm sure there is something you are not telling me."

"Sorry. Listen, you need to be on the lookout for anyone or anything out of the ordinary. We've really upset these Americans." Powell expected them to come after him hard and fast but in what guise he had no idea.

"What's happened?"

"Did you hear there was a bomb in London?"

"Yes, I heard about the suicide bombing," Afina confirmed.

"It didn't go down how it's being reported on the news."

"What do you mean?"

"Afina, the bomber was Lara," Powell explained gently. "Only she wasn't a bomber. They strapped a bomb to her and blew her up."

There was a stunned silence at the other end of the phone.

"I saw it on the news," Afina said hesitantly. "I had no idea it was Lara they were talking about." Powell could hear the crying at the end of the phone.

"I tried to stop them," Powell said. He was feeling guilty about his inability to save Lara. There was a growing list of women in his life, he'd been unable to save from a violent death. He had to protect Afina at all costs.

"Powell, who could do such a thing?"

"We know who is responsible. We don't know why but I intend to find out."

"I was so unfriendly to her," Afina sobbed.

"She never noticed," Powell lied. "Look, we'll be back at the bar soon. I'll explain what happened."

Powell used the remainder of the train journey to weigh up the options about what to do next. Clearly the sensible thing to do would be to emigrate to the other side of the world. He had no intention of making life so easy for Crawford and Barnes.

Powell knew he would do everything in his power to clear Lara's name. She did not deserve to be remembered as a terrorist. Neither should her father have to bear the stigma of his daughter being branded a terrorist. There were people who had been in Leicester Square who owed her their life. They had returned home to their loved ones because of her sacrifice. They needed to know she was not a terrorist.

He now had concrete information on those responsible for her death. He knew where the man calling himself Barnes lived and Crawford worked for the CIA. They could no longer hide from him but equally he lived his life out in the open. He couldn't just hide away and he would choose not to do so even if he could. He was easily found and he had no doubt they would come looking for him very soon.

Powell had suggested to Jenkins, he should head back to Wales and away from the danger. Jenkins agreed it was a sound idea and asked when they were both leaving, which ended the conversation. Powell was also concerned for Afina's safety. When he reached Brighton he was going to insist she take a holiday and go visit her family in Romania. It was the only way he could guarantee her safety.

By the time they arrived at the bar, Powell's head was aching and he was wondering if perhaps he should have stayed longer in hospital. Despite the warnings about alcohol, he went straight behind the bar and poured himself a large whisky.

Afina had been serving a table but hurried across once finished.

"I'm so sorry about Lara," Afina said. "What are you going to do?"

"The first thing I'm doing is closing the bar. Jenkins and I are going to be busy and I can't be worrying about the bar."

"I will look after the bar for you."

"I know you would Afina but I don't want them targeting the bar and innocent people getting killed. I want you to go stay with your mother and sister for a holiday. You haven't seen them for ages."

"You're trying to get rid of me."

"Absolutely. I want you safe and a long way from here. And this isn't up for debate. If you don't want to go see your family then go somewhere with Mara." Powell's tone didn't invite argument but still Afina looked doubtful. "Please Afina, just this once do as I ask."

"I will go see my family," she said, grudgingly. "My mother will be happy to see me. When are you going to close the restaurant?"

"After tonight. Please call everyone with a reservation, give them our apologies."

"What do I tell them?"

"Make something up. Then book a flight back home for tomorrow."

"I'll go start calling them," she said and walked away.

Jenkins had watched the conversation in silence. "She's not happy," he said.

"No but she will be safer back in Romania. I can't have her here. I worry too much about her."

Powell lifted the whisky bottle as if he was going to pour another drink.

"Drink anymore and you won't be fit for anything," Jenkins warned.

Powell put the bottle back down. "I guess you're right. Let's go to the office and work out our strategy."

CHAPTER FORTY THREE

Powell had shut the bar and he wasn't certain when, or if, it would ever be open again. Perhaps he was finally shutting the door on an earlier life. He no longer needed somewhere to hide away from life. There was no Bella to protect. He cared deeply for Afina but he had come to the view, she was only in danger as long as she spent time close to him. Afina was largely over her trafficking experience, she needed to be allowed to get on with her life. It was him and the bar which were holding her back.

Powell had insisted Afina spend the night away from the bar and as Mara would be working, she had agreed to spend the night at her friends, Emma and Becky.

"Still want to do this?" Jenkins asked, after Afina had left.

"I don't want to just sit around waiting for them to come for me."

"Okay. Then we should get going."

It was midnight and the journey would take about an hour. Jenkins was driving and the roads were empty. They took the A23 from Brighton, joined the M25 going west and turned north towards London on the A3.

They parked a short way down the road from where Barnes lived. They had no way of knowing if Barnes would be at home after everything that had happened but there was only one way to find out. Powell reasoned Barnes would expect him to still be in hospital or back in Brighton.

Barnes had no concrete reason to suspect that they knew where he lived. If he had discovered the bug Powell planted under his collar, which was unlikely, he wouldn't necessarily associate it with also being a GPS tracker.

There were no lights on in the house so he was either asleep or not at home. They walked purposefully up to the front door and as Powell picked the lock, Jenkins watched the street. Powell smiled as the door opened but then it was stopped from fully opening by a chain. He reached his arm inside the door and was just able to stretch far enough to release the chain. His smile returned as he stepped inside the house, closely followed by Jenkins.

Powell withdrew his gun from his coat pocket and they both stood still in the hallway, listening for any signs of life within the house. There was nothing to be detected but that wasn't really surprising if Barnes was asleep upstairs. He would have to be a very heavy snorer for the sound to reach downstairs.

Powell recognised that so far they had been lucky. The front door security was next to useless and there was no clever electronic surveillance in the hallway. Perhaps most importantly, Barnes wasn't a dog lover and they hadn't disturbed any family pet.

Powell signalled for Jenkins to follow and started to slowly climb the stairs. Fortunately, there were carpets on the stairs and no squeaky floorboards to give away their presence. They were soon on the upstairs landing. There were several doors leading off to the side. Powell ignored the first door to the side, which he considered likely to be a bathroom and put his ear to the next door. He could hear nothing and slowly turned the door handle. As he opened the door a few inches he could see a bedroom with a double bed but no sign of Barnes.

Powell moved to the next door feeling a sense of disappointment. The previous bedroom had looked like a master bedroom where he would have expected to find Barnes, if he was in the house. Powell quietly opened the second door a few inches and peered inside. There was another double bed but this time he could see someone was in the bed. Powell turned back to Jenkins and nodded to share his discovery.

Powell pushed the door open and moved closer to the bed. He had his gun held out in front, pointing at the person in the bed, who was covered by the duvet and not yet recognisable as Barnes. He moved close to the pillow and despite the darkness he could make out the features of a man with grey hair.

Powell turned back to Jenkins. "Turn on the light," he whispered.

Light flooded the room but Barnes took a moment to react. He gradually opened his eyes and was met with the sight of Powell and his weapon. He slowly sat up in bed without saying anything.

"Hello Barnes," Powell said. "Please don't make any sudden moves. We need to have a chat with you."

"You seem to have nine lives," Barnes replied.

"Is there anyone else in the house?"

"No."

Powell judged he was telling the truth. "Turn on your stomach and put your hands behind your back," he ordered.

Barnes did as instructed. Jenkins took the heavy duty duct tape from his pocket and wrapped it several times around Barnes's wrists, then stepped backwards.

"Jenkins, help him to sit up again," Powell suggested.

Jenkins helped to roughly pull Barnes in to a sitting position with his back resting against the headboard.

"What do you want?" Barnes asked.

"What do we want? How about the truth for a start. Why are you and Crawford promoting acts of terrorism?"

Barnes said nothing.

"I'm sorry," Powell apologised sarcastically. "I haven't introduced my friend. Barnes meet Jenkins. The interesting fact about Jenkins is he had a big time crush on Lara. He's an ex paratrooper and he came along tonight because I promised him the opportunity to meet the man responsible for Lara's death."

Jenkins withdrew a long knife from his belt and held it menacingly in his hand. Powell saw the first sign of fear in Barnes's eyes.

"It wasn't my idea."

"Well you didn't lift a finger to stop it happening, which to my mind makes you equally as guilty. There's also the small matter I was supposed to be blown up as well, which frankly means I would enjoy seeing Jenkins go to work on you with his knife." Powell let his words hang in the air for a minute. "So what I want to know is WHY? Why are you standing by while an American is setting off a bomb in the heart of London?"

Barnes took a few seconds while he seemed to be considering his options.

"Jenkins, remove one of his fingers to encourage him to answer quicker."

Jenkins forcefully took hold of Barnes's hand. "Stop moving or I'll take your whole bloody hand off," he warned.

"Wait, I'll tell you everything you want to know," Barnes begged, as Jenkins held the knife blade against his skin.

"I'm listening," Powell said.

Jenkins took a step back.

"The Americans are losing confidence in our commitment to fight terrorism. We are cutting back in every direction and that's under a Conservative government. If Labour come to power they will leave us defenceless. Something had to be done."

"And your answer is additional acts of terrorism? Are you mad?"

"Madness would be to do nothing."

"Well this madness has to stop before any more innocent people are killed… Does Crawford plan further attacks?"

"I'm not sure."

"I don't believe you," Powell said, raising his gun to point at Barnes. "Do you want me to let Jenkins loose on you?"

Barnes glanced at Jenkins and considered the idea for a second. "Crawford feels one more significant attack is necessary," he admitted.

"Which will be where?"

"I don't know."

Jenkins took a step nearer and raised his knife.

"Really I don't. Crawford doesn't feel I need to know." Barnes sounded a little desperate. "He works for the CIA. He thinks he's above the law."

"I just don't understand why someone who works for our government would allow the Americans to do this."

"It's because I work for our government, you fool."

Powell was taken aback by Barnes's response. "What do you mean exactly?"

"I work for the government. I do as I am instructed."

"Are you telling me that members of the government are aware of your actions?"

"They are more than just aware. This plan wasn't dreamed up by me and Crawford. We are simply implementing the plan."

CHAPTER FORTY FOUR

Powell couldn't believe what he was hearing. Surely Barnes must be lying to try and vindicate his actions. What worried Powell was the thought the plan went so high in government that no one could be trusted. Handing Barnes over to MI5 might achieve nothing and still leave himself exposed to danger.

"So who do you report to?" Powell asked.

"I report directly to the Home Secretary."

"Are you trying to tell me, the Home Secretary instructed you to carry out terrorist attacks in London?" Powell asked in disbelief.

"Not exactly. He informed me the Prime Minister had agreed to work with the Americans on a plan to garner support for the war against terror. They were fed up of being defeated in Parliament every time they tried to bring a bill to help combat terrorism."

Powell knew there was some truth in what Barnes said. The Prime Minister had introduced a bill to allow bombing of ISIS bases in Syria, which had been defeated. But this sounded too preposterous.

"I'm not sure I believe a word you're telling me," Powell said.

"Obviously, neither the Home Secretary or Prime Minister could be seen to be involved," Barnes continued. "I was told to take my orders from Crawford, with the understanding he had the full support of the Prime Minister."

"But did you really think the Prime Minister meant for you to bomb Londoners?"

"I questioned what Crawford was doing the first time I understood his intentions. And not particularly because I disagreed with his ideas but I wanted to make sure it was sanctioned. It was spelled out for me by the Home Secretary, they didn't want to know the details but I should do exactly as Crawford directed."

"Do you think it's right?"

"Right?" Barnes laughed. "I gave up many years ago questioning whether what I did was right. The people we elect get to make the decisions about what is right. I just do as I'm told."

"That hasn't worked as a defence since Nuremburg. Conspiring to kill innocent members of the public on British streets is murder. Pure and simple. There is no defence." Barnes attitude had infuriated Powell.

"Okay, so what should we do then?" Barnes snapped back. "My job is to protect the public from terrorism. I can't do that with a half-hearted government that refuses to invest properly in counter terrorism measures."

"Sounds to me like you are in favour of these attacks. You don't sound like someone just following orders."

"Yes, I am in favour. The government is already talking about doubling the investment in tackling ISIS. That would never have happened without these attacks. Whatever price has been paid has been worth it ten times over."

"But it hasn't been you paying the price. It's been innocent members of the public. If you believe so strongly in your actions, I'd respect you a lot more if I thought there was a chance in a million of you wearing a suicide vest. But there is no chance in hell of that happening. Is there?"

Barnes silence answered the question.

"Do you have any of this in writing?" Powell questioned.

"Of course I don't. It's not the sort of thing you'd want to fall into the wrong hands. I went to Eton with the Home Secretary. It is a simple matter of trust."

"Trust! The public put their trust in politicians and people like you, to act within the law. Government isn't meant to work on the foundation of old school networks."

"It's how things get done."

Powell still had one overriding concern. If Crawford was planning a further attack on London, he had to be stopped but that was easier said than done.

"Tell me, where is Al-Hashimi being held?" Powell asked.

"At my house in the country."

"Then I think we should pay a visit to your country house."

CHAPTER FORTY FIVE

Powell reasoned it would look extra suspicious turning up at Barnes's house in the middle of the night. It would be dangerous enough during the daytime. There were several of Crawford's men present and they would undoubtedly be on heightened alert after recent events. They may even have been warned about Powell and seen his photo. Powell hoped to avoid a bloodbath if at all possible.

According to Barnes's description of the house, it seemed more like a fortress, with impressive grounds surrounded by high fencing and CCTV everywhere. Barnes would be able to provide entry through the outer gate but as they approached the house itself, they could expect a reception committee of one or more armed men. Powell was hoping the presence of Barnes would give them the advantage of surprise and they could disarm Crawford's men with the minimum fuss. He was always an optimist.

The questioning of Barnes went on most of the night. The first question was to ask him his real name. He had said it was David Gregory but Powell wasn't entirely convinced. The credit cards in Barnes's wallet were all in the name of Barnes. There was nothing in the house to prove his name one way or another. Barnes real name was no longer of interest to Powell. Once Barnes was handed over to MI5, they would be able to discover his real identity.

It seemed certain there was a conspiracy that reached to the heart of government but proving anything would be more difficult. Powell had no doubt that if Barnes was ever let free, he would simply recant everything he had admitted. There was no proof and Barnes would no doubt say he was telling a pack of lies, while being threatened by two armed madmen. Even with Barnes testimony, the politicians would deny their involvement. The story sounded so farfetched, it would take concrete evidence to convince anyone of their guilt.

Powell wanted to get his hands on Al-Hashimi. Brian had assured him the Director General would act if he had sufficient evidence and Al-Hashimi was part of that evidence. Throw in Barnes, who Brian could testify to being in Leicester Square with Crawford at the time of Lara's explosion and it started to build a case. It may not add up to a watertight case in a court of law but this was not a matter that was likely to end up in a public trial. He didn't need evidence that was admissible in a court, just strong enough to make the DG investigate. The results may never see the light of day but action would be taken.

The problem was that the Director General had been warned by the Home Secretary to forget Lara's claims about Al-Hashimi. Whatever his true name, he was only a small cog in ISIS and MI6 along with the Americans had the matter in hand. The Director General was a career member of MI5 who had climbed the ranks. He didn't take kindly to being told how to do his job by a politician but neither did he intend to put his job on the line without evidence. He needed something concrete to be able to thwart the influence being exerted.

Brian arrived at the house at seven in the morning to ferry them to Barnes's house in Kent. Barnes was made to get dressed while Jenkins watched, much to his annoyance. Not that Jenkins was a voyeur, he just had to make sure Barnes didn't have any hidden weapons in the bedroom. Powell made fresh coffee in the kitchen and when Barnes appeared, Powell went back up to the bedroom and recovered the listening device from the lapel of Barnes's jacket, which was hanging in a wardrobe. It was too valuable to leave behind.

When Powell returned downstairs it was time to leave. Brian had one man with him, who he trusted implicitly and introduced as O'Neill. If the name hadn't been enough of a clue, there was no doubt about his Irish heritage once he spoke. They were both armed and brought with them some additional items they felt were necessary for the job in hand. Jenkins was armed with the weapon taken from Brown, which meant there were now four of them armed if events turned nasty.

One of the most important items brought by Brian was the disposable, transparent gloves, which would ensure they left no fingerprints. All of their fingerprints were a matter of record and they didn't want them being found anywhere in Barnes's country house and the police ending up arresting them for a crime. Especially as the crime could be murder, if they had to shoot any of the Americans protecting Al-Hashimi.

Barnes was bundled into the back of the Volvo between O'Neill and Jenkins. Brian drove and Powell sat next to him in the front. The roads were busy and it took almost two hours before they reached the vicinity of their destination. They stopped for a minute and Barnes was made to swap seats with Powell. Barnes was the senior man present and it would look more natural him sitting in the front. Powell made him aware Jenkins would shoot him in the back of the head at the first sign of him not cooperating.

CHAPTER FORTY SIX

They drove up to the gate and Barnes told Brian the number to enter in to the security system, which led to the gate swinging open. They moved forward cautiously. They expected someone was watching them on CCTV and possibly getting nervous about their sudden intrusion. As they came close to the house, Powell could see two men emerge with automatic weapons. They watched like hawks as Brian brought the car to a stop. Both men had their weapons trained on the car.

Barnes stepped out first with Powell close behind. They kept their hands in view and moved slowly so as not to invite trouble. Barnes was just as careful as Powell because he realised, he was equally in danger of getting shot.

"Who are you?" one of the men with a gun asked, in an American accent and none too politely. "This is a restricted area. Who gave you the entry key?"

Powell realised it was the fact they knew the entry number that would stop the armed men from acting rashly. For all they knew, these new arrivals were important.

"This is my house," Barnes answered. "I'm having my own meeting. It's not for your exclusive bloody use." He started to walk towards the front door.

By now, Jenkins and O'Neill were also out of the car. Brian was planning to stay seated in case they needed an urgent getaway.

"Wait a minute," the man with the automatic said, pointing his weapon at Barnes and blocking his path. "No one goes inside this house without my boss telling me it's okay. I don't care who you are."

"Then I suggest you give Crawford a call."

Powell could see that Barnes familiar use of Crawford's name made the man relax a little.

"Watch them," the man instructed, taking his phone from his pocket. He held it to his ear and placed the call.

Powell had disarmed him of his phone and weapon before he knew what had hit him. Powell kicked him in the groin and then swept his legs away. In the same moment Jenkins dealt with the other man. They had agreed beforehand that they couldn't allow anyone to speak with Crawford. He would immediately smell a rat.

O'Neill had his weapon covering both of the men on the ground. Jenkins picked up the automatic weapons and put them to the side. Then he tied each man's hands behind their backs with plastic ties. He put his pistol away and picked up the automatic weapons. He looked as if he had won the lottery, the way he was admiring his new weapon. He offered the second automatic weapon to Powell, who nodded his refusal.

Powell preferred his pistol. He hoped not to have to shoot anyone and as he hadn't handled an automatic weapon for over twenty years, didn't think this was the time to start using an unfamiliar weapon. He was averse to the idea of killing anyone if it could be avoided. These men were just following orders and almost certainly didn't understand the bigger picture. It was Crawford, Barnes and the politicians he held responsible for Lara's death.

"I'll take that, if it's going free?" O'Neill asked and Jenkins handed him the weapon.

"How many men are there inside?" Powell asked the American who had earlier blocked their entrance.

The man was slow to respond and O'Neill used the butt of his weapon to hit him on the side of the head. "He asked you a question," he emphasised, threatening to hit him again.

"There's five of us in total."

That was the number Barnes had mentioned but Powell was pleased to receive confirmation. Only three more men remained inside and they were now outnumbered. Powell didn't want to spend any longer out in the open, especially as there was the possibility they were already being observed on CCTV.

"You two on your feet," Powell instructed. O'Neill and Jenkins helped them stand up.

"Jenkins, go around the back and try to check out what's waiting for us on the other side of the door. I'll give you a couple of minutes then we're coming in."

Jenkins hurried away. They had all been briefed on the layout of the house by Barnes and knew there was a rear entrance through the kitchen.

"Barnes, you are going to wait in the car with Brian," Powell said.

He followed behind Barnes and watched him carefully until he was sat in the back seat. Brian turned around and aimed his weapon between Barnes's eyes.

"It's time," Powell announced, returning to the front door and checking his watch. "You're going first through the door," he informed the two Americans.

O'Neill prodded them both in the back with his weapon. They seemed less than enthusiastic to go through the door.

"Looks like we can expect trouble," Powell warned. "O'Neill, shoot them if they aren't through the door within the next five seconds."

The first American steeped inside the house but at the same time threw himself to the ground. "Don't shoot, it's me," he screamed.

O'Neill used the second American as cover, as he shoved him through the door. There was immediate gunfire from within the house and the American fell to the ground. O'Neill returned fire in the general direction of the gun shots at the same time as he dived to his left.

Powell entered crouched low and moved to the right. He caught a glimpse of the man who was focused on firing at O'Neill from the top of the stairs. Powell fired two shots in quick succession and the man tumbled down the stairs.

O'Neill regained his feet and stood ready to respond to any new sign of danger. The American who had been first through the door was trying to crawl away and O'Neill walked across to him and hit him none too gently on the bag of the head with his weapon.

There were further shots from the rear of the house.

"There should be two more of them," Powell said. "It sounds like Jenkins may need our help."

Powell headed towards the sound of the continuous gunfire, followed by O'Neill. There was a long kitchen and dining room at the back and to one side of the house. Powell poked his head around the door and could see the back of someone behind the dining table firing at Jenkins, who was using the kitchen worktable as cover.

"Drop your weapon," Powell commanded, stepping into the room.

The man in front froze, knowing he was an easy target. He placed his gun on the wooden floor.

"Slide the weapon away from you," Powell instructed.

The man did as ordered and put his hands on the back of his neck.

Jenkins stood up and approached Powell. "Sorry about that," Jenkins said. "I was supposed to be watching your back not the other way around."

Powell smiled. "No problem. There is one of them left, who is probably in the basement guarding Al-Hashimi. You take care of this one and then check on the state of the ones in the entrance hall, who have been shot. Once we are clear of here we can call for an ambulance. O'Neill and I will go find Al-Hashimi and the last American."

CHAPTER FORTY SEVEN

Powell had learned from Barnes that Al-Hashimi was being interrogated in the large basement and the entrance was from a door off the hallway, close to the kitchen. Powell positioned himself on one side of the door and O'Neill on the other. Powell turned the handle and pushed the door open with his foot, quickly stepping back.

The stairs leading down to the basement were well lit and anyone entering was going to be an easy target. There was no sound from below. Powell hoped Al-Hashimi hadn't been moved.

"Keep watch for a minute," Powell said to O'Neill.

Powell returned to the kitchen to find Jenkins pulling the American to his feet with his hands tied behind his back.

"What's the name of the man downstairs?" Powell asked.

"George."

"What's your name?"

"Andy."

"Well Andy, I'd like you to persuade George to give us Al-Hashimi. If we have to go down after him, George is going to end up dead. I'd like to avoid that scenario if possible."

"You mean you'd like to avoid getting shot yourself," the man said with a smirk.

"That's true," Powell agreed. "But you owe me. I could have simply shot you in the back but I didn't. We just want Al-Hashimi and there's been enough blood shed."

Powell grabbed Andy by the arm and pulled him toward the entrance to the basement. Powell positioned him at the top of the stairs in the open doorway.

"George," Powell called out. "I've got your friend Andy here. I don't mean you any harm. I just want Al-Hashimi. Send him up here and we'll be on our way."

There was no response from the basement.

"Andy, please tell George to give us Al-Hashimi," Powell said in an even tone. "Otherwise you're going to be our human shield as we go down there."

Andy's eyes said he didn't like the idea of being first in to the basement.

"George, it's me, Andy. We're the only two left. Send up Al-Hashimi. He's not worth getting killed for."

George spoke for the first time. "Let them try and take him."

Powell looked at O'Neill. "Ready?" he asked.

O'Neill nodded.

Powell took Andy by the collar of his jacket and using him as a shield, edged slowly down a couple of stairs.

"George, don't shoot," Andy begged.

O'Neill lay himself on the ground and lying on his stomach slid down the first couple of stairs, gaining a clear view of the room below for the first time. He was barely visible to George and anyway his attention would be on Powell and Andy.

George was pointing his pistol at the two men inching their way down the stairs. "Don't come any further or I'll shoot you both," George warned.

"Don't do that, George," Powell replied. "If you start firing you're going to end up dead."

"Fuck you," George shouted and fired.

Powell felt Andy's body go limp and he let him drop to the ground and fall down the stairs. He brought his weapon up to return fire but the danger was already over. George hadn't noticed O'Neill in the tangle of legs. He had instantly returned fire and George dropped to the ground.

Powell rushed down the stairs to George's body, his weapon held out in front ready to fire if necessary. George's gun had fallen at his side and Powell kicked it out of harm's way.

"You should have listened to me, George," Powell said.

George was clutching at a wound in his chest. He wasn't dead but he looked in a bad way and wasn't going to cause any more trouble.

O'Neill was standing over the body of Andy. "This one will live," he said. "Just caught him in the shoulder."

For the first time, Powell could see deep within the basement and at one end was a man sitting on a camp bed looking expectantly in his direction. Then Powell noticed the chains from his ankles to the wall. His hands were also handcuffed behind his back.

"Secure all the Americans," Powell instructed. "Then we need to get out of here before Crawford sends reinforcements. They must have let him know they were under attack. Fortunately, we're in the middle of nowhere so hopefully there won't be anyone getting here anytime too soon."

Powell walked towards Al-Hashimi. As he came near, there was a rancid smell in the air. Close to the bed was a metal bucket, which smelt of human waste. Al-Hashimi looked in a terrible mess. His beard was unkempt and his hair looked greasy. His face was covered with bright blue and yellow bruises and he was missing a large part of both ears and some teeth.

Powell shuddered to imagine what the rest of his body must look like under his clothes. Lara had described how Brown had mutilated his manhood and he felt a moment's sympathy for the man, before reminding himself this was the same man who had carried out the London Marathon bombing.

"You're coming with us," Powell explained. "Do as I say and I promise there will be no further torture."

Al-Hashimi showed little sign of emotion. His will had been broken as well as his body. His eyes stared straight ahead, dark pools of despair.

"Who are you?" Al-Hashimi asked.

"My name is Powell. We are going to take you somewhere safe."

Al-Hashimi summoned up some strength. "I hope you killed all of them," he said.

Powell ignored the comment and walked over to George. His breathing was laboured and he was coughing up drops of blood. Powell reckoned he'd been shot in the lung and he was now drowning in his own blood.

"Where are the keys?" Powell asked.

George was too preoccupied with his pain to care about keys. Powell bent down and searched his pockets. George grabbed his wrist. "Please finish me," he croaked, holding on surprisingly tightly.

Powell removed George's hand and extracted a set of keys from George's pocket. He felt sympathy for George. Unlike Al-Hashimi, he wasn't a terrorist. He may well have a wife and children at home. Who knows what story he'd been fed by Crawford. He was probably just a grunt thinking he was fighting terrorism. It was always the grunts who paid the price for the ambition of men in loftier positions.

"I'm sorry," Powell said and turned away, although not before he'd seen the look of despair on the man's face.

He soon had Al-Hashimi free of his leg chains. He could remain handcuffed.

"I hope he takes a long time to die," Al-Hashimi said, sitting on his bed, staring coldly at George. He spat on the floor.

Powell knew where his sympathies belonged. He took two paces towards George and shot him in the head.

CHAPTER FORTY EIGHT

Al-Hashimi had needed to be supported to make it up the stairs. His feet had been severely beaten and he couldn't walk. Despite his obvious pain, he remained silent. Powell reasoned he hadn't been an easy man to break. Perhaps the extreme nature of the torture he'd undergone was simply testament to Al-Hashimi's bravery, rather than a barbaric blood lust on the part of Brown.

Powell found the study where Barnes said the CCTV was controlled and removed the current disc. There was a box of further discs to the side. Each disc was marked with a date and time. They were obviously the tapes of Al-Hashimi being interrogated. They would make excellent evidence. Perhaps Barnes or Crawford would feature on the tapes. He carried the box under his arm and headed for the car.

By the time he arrived back at the car, Jenkins and O'Neill were bundling Al-Hashimi into the boot. There were no protests from the terrorist. For all he knew, Powell would resort to new methods of torture if he didn't do exactly as he was told. He was in no state to argue or resist. Powell took the front passenger seat while O'Neill and Jenkins sandwiched Barnes on the back seat. Brian accelerated away and Powell breathed a sigh of relief they had all made it out of the house in one piece.

"Al-Hashimi looks in a bad way," Jenkins commented. "He needs medical treatment."

"He'll get some soon, just not today," Powell responded.

"You will all be needing medical treatment soon," Barnes interjected. "That's in the unlikely event any of you are still alive by this time tomorrow."

Jenkins gave Barnes a hard dig in his ribs with an elbow. "Be sure of one thing. If I'm not alive tomorrow, then neither will you be."

"Don't drive so fast," Powell cautioned Brian. "We don't want to get stopped for speeding."

Brian slowed a little. "Just trying to put some distance between us and the house," he explained.

"Where are we going?" O'Neill asked.

"Maidenhead. I know someone with a large house, who can be discrete."

"I hope we're doing the right thing going to Samurai's house," Brian said. "We could be bringing a ton of trouble down on his head."

"You may be right," Powell conceded. "But we have few options. We can't return to Brighton or trust any of your safe houses."

"Samurai! That sounds an interesting name," O'Neill remarked.

"He's a computer hacker," Powell replied. "And a very good one."

"Does he know what he's getting into?" Brian asked.

"Once I explained what happened to Lara and our suspicions about the Americans, he was desperate to help. You have to remember, he's very anti-establishment."

Powell had deep misgivings about involving Samurai and more importantly his sister, who by accident of birth alone was trespassing on the wrong side of the law. Tina had seemed very normal and poles apart from her brother in terms of lifestyle. Powell had suggested she should take an immediate holiday at his expense but she had refused. If her brother was about to become involved in something that was obviously dangerous, then she would be going nowhere. Interestingly, she hadn't sought to dissuade her brother from providing help. She had actually told Powell she trusted his judgement on moral issues and would support his decision.

Powell waited until they were on the M25 before placing a call to the emergency services using the phone they had taken from Barnes. He kept it short but asked for police and ambulances, explaining there had been a gunfight leaving several casualties. Once he had finished the call, he turned the phone off so it couldn't be traced.

They arrived at the large, detached house on the outskirts of Maidenhead without incident. They turned into the circular driveway in front of the house and parked behind the detached double garage to the side, which meant they were hidden out of view from the road.

As they climbed from the car, the front door was already open and Tina was surveying her visitors. O'Neill and Jenkins made little attempt to hide their weapons and Powell could see the surprise on Tina's face as they roughly pushed Barnes towards the house followed by Brian.

Powell strode up to Tina with what he hoped was a comforting smile. "It's good to see you again," he said. "Sorry about the circumstances."

Tina held the front door open as everyone trooped inside the house. "I thought you said there would be six of you," she queried.

"There's one more in the boot of the car," Powell answered.

Tina gave him a quizzical look. "Are you going to get him?" she asked.

Powell was impressed that Tina took everything so calmly. "O'Neill, you and Jenkins bring him in. I'll watch Barnes." Turning back to Tina he asked, "Can you show us to a bedroom. The new man is quite badly injured."

"Do you know I'm a nurse?" she asked suspiciously.

Powell decided he didn't want to lie. "It came up when I first did business with your brother." In truth, he had Brian check her out after their first meeting and discovered that despite her brother's strange profession, she was indeed a nurse on a paediatric ward.

They all watched as Al-Hashimi was supported under each arm and brought into the house.

"Bring him upstairs," Tina said. "The rest of you can go through to the lounge."

Powell showed Brian and Barnes the way to the lounge.

"Where's Samurai," Brian asked.

"He has an office at the bottom of the garden," Powell explained. "I suspect he spends most of his life there."

Tina joined them in the lounge after a few minutes. "Who did that to him?" she asked angrily.

"The men we are hiding from," Powell replied.

"Save your sympathy," Barnes said. "He's a bloody terrorist. He wouldn't think twice about beheading you."

"He's a human being," Tina retorted.

"He's right," Powell said. "He is a terrorist and probably responsible for the London marathon bombing."

"I expect terrorists to blow people up," Tina said. "I thought the rest of us behaved differently."

"Most of us are different," Powell agreed. Unfortunately the minority still amounted to a very significant number of people.

He shared Tina's sentiment about what was right and wrong. Broadly speaking, he believed there were lines a government shouldn't cross. However, he also knew, if he was being completely honest, that if someone he loved was in danger, he would do absolutely anything necessary, without a second thought, to save them including torturing someone. He was open to being called a hypocrite but believed there was a difference. The state wielded too much power to be allowed to operate outside the law because then they could not be held accountable. If an individual acted outside the law then he was answerable to the laws of the land for his actions.

"It's that sort of weak willed thinking, which allows terrorism to flourish," Barnes argued.

"You can keep quiet. Otherwise I'll gag you," Powell threatened.

"Who is he?" Tina asked.

"He works for our government doing the dirty jobs they like to keep secret. He is one of the men responsible for what happened to the man upstairs but I believe he is also part of a conspiracy, working with the Americans, to commit acts of terrorism in the belief it will make us want to support putting troops on the ground in the Middle East."

Tina stared at Barnes as if he was the devil. "Haven't you people learned anything from history?" she asked.

"I heard you say you're a nurse," Barnes replied coldly. "You should understand the need to cut out the cancer before it spreads."

"Is your brother down the garden?" Powell asked, keen to change the subject.

"Yes and he's expecting you. I'm going to try and make the man upstairs more comfortable. Shout if you need anything."

"Brian and I will take Barnes to see your brother. Please be careful with your patient. He is a fanatic and still potentially dangerous. Listen to what O'Neill and Jenkins tell you."

"I'll be careful," Tina agreed. "But I don't think he's dangerous anymore."

CHAPTER FORTY NINE

Powell spent almost two hours with Samurai, before they were both finally happy with the results of their work. It turned out Samurai was quite adept at writing and had no problem massaging the information Powell provided into a coherent story. Brian and Jenkins provided additional details and Barnes contributed unwillingly by having his photo taken. They also took photos of Al-Hashimi.

Powell picked a couple of the discs from the box he'd recovered from the house, which he thought covered the dates when Al-Hashimi was being tortured. He was grateful for the changes in technology, which meant he could now view the recordings of what took place in the house, directly on a computer. It had been very different in his youth when old fashioned video tapes were the norm.

Powell warned Samurai, what they were about to watch would be very graphic. They all gathered around the screen. No one said anything and the only sounds in the room were Al-Hashimi's screams. Halfway through the second disc, Samurai ran outside the office and threw up in the garden. Powell wasn't surprised. Despite knowing what to expect, his stomach still turned at the site of Brown's torturing methods. Brian and Jenkins hid their emotions behind passive faces.

"I think that's more than enough," Powell said. "Those files added to everything else we have should get people's attention."

"I felt like I was watching one of those ISIS videos they publish on the Internet," Jenkins said. "Where they burn people alive or drown them."

"This is going to cause a terrible stink," Brian said. "It will make great propaganda for the terrorists. We may even be putting the lives of our people at risk. You can imagine ISIS wanting to retaliate in kind."

"Are you saying we shouldn't include these recordings?" Powell asked. "They are the strongest proof we have of a crime being committed as what Brown is doing is illegal. It also supports our claims about the American involvement as you can hear their accents."

"I'm not saying we shouldn't publish the recordings," Brian backtracked.

"Just that we can expect them to be used against the West."

"What do you others think?" Powell asked.

"They add a lot of weight to our story," Jenkins replied. "I don't think we have much choice."

"I agree," Samurai said. "This sort of abuse by our government needs to be exposed."

"Then we are all agreed," Powell summarised. "Anyway, this is still only our backup plan. If all goes well and the DG takes action, none of this will ever see the light of day."

"I think he will have to act after he sees this," Brian said, confidently.

"I have everything I need," Samurai said. "You all go back to the house and leave me to get on with things. I'll need at least a couple of hours."

Back in the house, Powell had Jenkins put a gag in Barnes's mouth, as his inability to keep quiet finally tested Powell's patience one too many times. They had left him tied to a chair and Tina admitted she was close to cutting out his tongue.

Jenkins and O'Neill took turns watching Al-Hashimi, who had said very little and surprisingly seemed to have no interest in finding out who it was that now held him prisoner and what his future held. Perhaps he was just happy to be away from the men who had caused him so much pain and suffering.

Tina announced she planned to cook a simple pasta meal and Powell offered to make a salad. They were waiting for Samurai to tell them he was ready and Powell needed to do something to occupy himself.

"You know the work Samurai does is dangerous," Powell commented, as he washed the salad leaves. "One day he is going to upset the wrong people and they will come looking for him."

"Is that a veiled warning about what you are asking him to do?"

"Once he has published our story, if it comes to that, I don't think they will bother with him. The cat will be out of the bag and they would have nothing to gain. In fact, they would risk drawing more attention to themselves and these people don't like being in the spotlight. Of course, if they knew what he was planning to do, it would be a different matter. They would stop at nothing to prevent his publishing our story."

"It's that important?"

"Yes. But I was thinking more generally about the work he does. Upsetting large pharmaceutical companies and taking on the banks, for example, can be dangerous… And I'm worried you might get hurt because of what he does." Powell knew Samurai had been campaigning against drug testing on animals and bankers illegally manipulating markets.

"I've always understood what he does is not only illegal but potentially dangerous. But I believe in my brother and he always does things for a good reason. He's not one of these hackers who publishes people's credit card details just for the fun. He sees himself as a moral crusader. That's why he offered you, his help."

"And I'm very grateful. I don't know what I would have done without his help. But I also feel guilty about involving you in something so dangerous."

"It was our decision. You didn't hold a gun to our heads."

"Just take care. I wouldn't cope very well if anything bad happened to either of you."

"That goes both ways. It's not often I get to meet someone with a real backbone. Too many people do what is easy rather than what's right."

"I'm just an awkward sod."

Tina poured pasta into a pan of boiling water. "You seem quite domesticated," she said, noticing how he was efficiently chopping the salad.

"I've run a bar in Brighton, which sells decent food, for twenty years now. When a chef goes sick it can be all hands to the pump. You must come and visit us one day."

"It will have to be a long time in the future. It's probably best not to be seen together, if what you are about to publish is as important as you say."

"Pity. I would have liked to see you again."

"And I would have liked to see you again, Powell. You're an interesting man."

Once the food was ready, they placed everything on the dining table and everyone took turns helping themselves to what they wanted. Powell had Tina take some food up to Al-Hashimi. Barnes had his gag removed and Tina fed him some pasta without his complaining.

Just as Powell was becoming restless with waiting, Samurai walked into the lounge and announced everything was in place. He had only to press one key and every television station, news site, blogger and a host of important individuals including Members of Parliament, would receive a file containing the details of everything from Lara learning about Al-Hashimi to the present time. There were also photos of Al-Hashimi and Barnes attached to the file as well as the video recordings.

Powell and Lara had been given pseudonyms in the report, which could invite accusations it was unsubstantiated nonsense from someone with an axe to grind. But there was no way Powell was going to invite the world to examine every detail of his life by using his real name. Samurai had a good reputation based on his previous work and was known only to publish accurate information. Anything he published would have instant credibility.

Once Samurai lit the touch paper, there could be no going back. The story would be quickly global and the government would be unable to suppress the details. There would no doubt be character attacks on everyone from Samurai to the mystery individuals described in the report but questions would be asked and a good investigative journalist, with the bit between his teeth, should be able to shake the trees enough to cause problems for the guilty.

Powell was satisfied with his backup plan and it was time to ask Brian to contact his Director General and set in motion the preferred plan. If the next twenty four hours didn't go according to plan, Powell trusted Samurai to flood the Internet with the story and it would be some form of revenge, even if he wasn't around any longer to see the fallout.

Powell's phone rang and he was surprised to see it was Afina calling.

CHAPTER FIFTY

Crawford responded quickly to the realisation Al-Hashimi had been taken. He'd received the call telling him a car was approaching the house and the driver knew the code so assumed it must be Barnes. He was the only other person who knew the code. Although not happy about his sudden visit, the man did own the house and no doubt had some reason for his unplanned visit.

Crawford expected a further call to confirm the purpose of Barnes's visit but the call never came. He tried phoning the team at the house but there was no answer and there could only be one reason, the team had been taken out. He then tried calling Barnes but again there was no answer. He was either turning his back on his erstwhile partner out of choice or being forced to cooperate. The latter option seemed more likely.

Crawford was in a helicopter with a new team and circling the house within the hour. The presence of police cars and ambulances down below led him to abandon the idea of landing. It had to be the work of Powell and Crawford knew his operation was close to collapse.

He started making calls to ensure he was updated on what the police discovered. The most damning evidence in the house, was the video recordings. If he was Powell, he would have taken them. They supported his story and gave him leverage. On the positive side, it would mean the local police weren't already in possession of the tapes.

Everything else at the house could be explained away as a CIA safe house, which had been attacked, possibly by terrorists. If not terrorists, then perhaps a drug Lord seeking revenge. The police would be wanting to speak with Barnes, as the owner of the house. His disappearance made everything more difficult. He would be able to close the investigation and also ensure there was only minimal coverage in the newspapers. Without Barnes, explanations were infinitely more complicated.

Crawford needed to urgently find Powell. He certainly hadn't acted alone but Crawford was confident if he found Powell, he would find Al-Hashimi and Barnes. He needed to find them before events spiralled completely out of control. If Powell handed Al-Hashimi over to MI5, all hell would break loose.

Crawford directed the helicopter pilot to fly to Brighton and they landed at nearby Shoreham airport. They took a taxi to Powell's bar only to find it closed. Crawford was pretty sure it confirmed Powell was responsible for the attack on the house and was in hiding. They would go check out where he lived but he wasn't hopeful of finding anyone at home. Crawford realised he was guilty of underestimating Powell. He wouldn't repeat the mistake.

Having discovered an empty house, Crawford frantically racked his brain for what to do next. The simplest plans were usually the best. He urgently needed to get his hands on someone close to Powell. He needed a bargaining chip.

Crawford had thoroughly researched Powell after Brown's failures, which was how he knew about the death of Powell's daughter. He had read the police reports and hacked his emails. They revealed little of interest at the time but now he was recalling the email Powell sent to his lawyer telling him, in the event of his death, he wanted everything left to someone called Afina. She was the same girl who had cropped up in police reports. Powell obviously cared deeply for her and she worked in his bar. Powell must have sent her away for her own safety. He needed to find her and quickly.

CHAPTER FIFTY ONE

Afina was looking forward to visiting her mother and sister. She had seen them at Christmas in Brighton but it had been more than six months since she was last in Bucharest. Her view of her homeland had changed since living in England. She could no longer see herself moving back to Romania to live permanently and had told her mother so at Christmas, which led to an argument and tears.

Previously, Afina had always told her mother she would just work in England for a couple of years, to make some money and then she would return to Romania. She tried to explain to her mother, there were few jobs in Bucharest and none of them paid a fraction of what she could earn in England.

Afina knew she was being selfish by remaining in Brighton when her mother wanted her to return to Bucharest but for the first time in her life, she had found her vocation. She liked running the bar and she loved Brighton. It wasn't just for financial reasons she wanted to remain. Brighton was far more cosmopolitan than Bucharest. In Brighton you could be anyone and do anything without attracting adverse comments. She was sure she could have a great future in Brighton, which she didn't feel about Bucharest. One day she would like to own a bar in Brighton.

Afina had always been close to her mother and there argument at Christmas had left her feeling guilty. What made matters worse was that Afina knew her sister planned to come to England as soon as she was eighteen, which was only a year away.

Afina wanted her mother to come and live in Brighton but she didn't speak English and she had friends she had known all her life in Bucharest. She was adamant she didn't want to live anywhere but Romania. Afina knew there was little chance of changing her mother's mind.

Afina had enjoyed spending the previous night with Emma and Becky. They had been a lifeline when she was first in Brighton and she would never forget their kindness to a complete stranger. They had gone out for a meal at a Thai restaurant in Kemptown. Afina had become used to eating so many different types of food since being in Brighton. Before arriving in England she had never eaten any Asian food. After a great meal, they went to their favourite bar and Mara joined them for a couple of hours at the end of the evening. They all drank copious amounts of wine and ended the evening with shots, which had left Afina feeling a little delicate come the morning.

She arrived early at the airport for her afternoon flight. Having checked in online and taking only hand baggage for what she envisaged would be a short trip, she joined the queue at Departures, ready to show her boarding pass and passport. She smiled at the man seated at the desk and handed him her documents. She was thinking about the coffee she planned to get as soon as she was through the security checks.

The man held her passport face down on his screen and then looked up at her, before once again looking at his screen. He turned his head to the side and gave a small indication to two men standing nearby.

Afina was wondering why it was taking longer than usual when she noticed the two men approach. The man at the desk handed her passport to a man in a grey suit. The other man was more casually dressed in jeans and a shirt.

"Excuse me, Miss. Will you please come with us," the man in the suit requested politely but firmly.

"What's the problem?" Afina asked. "It's not out of date."

"Please just come with us," the grey suit repeated.

Afina saw little point in arguing and was becoming conscious she was holding up the queue. "Okay," she agreed.

The suit led the way to a small office. Afina noticed how the man in the jeans walked behind her as if blocking any attempt on her part to turn and run away.

"Please take a seat, Miss," the suit directed. "I'm Inspector Davies. May I call you Afina?"

Afina nodded her agreement.

"Do you know someone called Stefan?" Davies continued.

"What is this about?"

"Please just answer the question."

Afina shuddered at the memories. "Yes," she answered simply. She was wondering where this questioning would lead.

"We have reason to believe you engaged with this Stefan in the trafficking of young girls for the purpose of prostitution."

"Are you mad," Afina exclaimed. "I was one of the girls trafficked. The police in Brighton know this."

"I understand some new evidence has come to light. My colleague will be taking you to Brighton police station for further questioning."

"But what about my flight?"

"I'm afraid you won't be catching any flight today."

"Can I make a phone call?" Afina asked.

"All in good time."

"I want to make a call now," Afina demanded. "I need to let my mother know I'm not on the flight."

"That will be possible once we get you to the station," the man in jeans replied, speaking for the first time.

"I'm going nowhere until I make a call," Afina insisted. She sat back and crossed her arms.

"The sooner you go with my colleague, the sooner this can be sorted out and you can make your phone call," Davies said pleasantly. "Otherwise, we will put you in the local cells until you agree to be more helpful. It's your choice. We're in no desperate hurry."

Afina could see nothing she said would change their minds. She stood up and said, "Okay, let's get on with it."

The man in jeans, who still hadn't given his name, escorted her through a part of the airport the public didn't normally get to see. After a few minutes, they emerged on to a quiet road where a black car with tinted windows was waiting. She thought it was a BMW but wasn't certain. Two men stepped out from the car.

One of the men opened the rear door for her to get in. She was reluctant for a second. Something didn't seem right. For a start, it wasn't a police car and the men weren't wearing police uniforms. They were dressed in dark suits. They reminded her of the three men who came to the bar for Lara.

"Please get in the car," one of the men said, seeing her hesitancy.

As soon as she heard the American accent, she instinctively started to run but the man in the jeans was too quick for her and grabbed her from behind. He pushed her towards the car.

Powell had taught her a few simple self-defence moves. She kicked backwards with all her strength, aiming for his knee but hitting him in the shin instead.

He swore and loosened his grip.

She pulled her arms free and was intending to run but the man who had opened the rear car door was now in front of her.

She saw the blow coming towards her but couldn't get out of the way. She was stunned and fell backwards into the arms of the man in jeans. She didn't resist further as the two men bundled her into the back of the car.

The man in jeans watched the car drive away, then turned and walked back inside the airport. He wondered what the girl had done to make such powerful enemies.

CHAPTER FIFTY TWO

Powell was shocked the second he heard Crawford's voice calling from Afina's phone. He was also immediately deeply concerned. It could only mean one thing and his mind immediately flashed back to thoughts of Lara. He could not allow the same end result.

"Powell, you will do exactly as I say or you won't see your friend Afina again. Actually, that isn't true. I'm going to give her to Brown as a gift, video their time together and send you a copy of the video as a present. It will be a lasting memory of your foolishness."

"I want to speak to her," Powell replied without emotion.

"Of course you do."

There was a moment's silence before Afina came on the line. "Powell, I'm okay. I've told them you will kill every one of them if they don't let me go..."

Powell could hear the phone being snatched from Afina's grasp and her being dragged away screaming obscenities.

"She has spirit. I will give her that," Crawford said. "And she seems to have great belief in you. I don't think she really appreciates the reality of the situation. But you do, don't you Powell?"

"I understand that if you harm her, you are a dead man." Out of the corner of his eye, he could see Brian and Tina attentively listening to his conversation. They realised there was a problem.

"I don't think you are in a position to make threats," Crawford said. "Not if you truly value Afina's life."

"You don't hold all the cards," Powell answered. "I have Al-Hashimi and Barnes. The only way you get them back is in exchange for a healthy Afina."

"Afina has not been harmed. I believed her when she said she didn't know where you are staying. You are too clever to tell her your plans so I have not wasted time on interrogating her."

Powell remembered Afina asking about his plan and her not being convinced it was for her own good that she knew nothing. She had suggested he didn't trust her and not been happy.

"Crawford, I warn you. Ignore the idea in your head that you are going to kill me at our rendezvous and walk away with what you want. It isn't going to happen. It's a fair exchange or nothing."

"You aren't very trusting, Powell. I need Al-Hashimi and Barnes back more than I need you dead. I also want the discs with the recordings of Al-Hashimi's interrogation. I presume you have them?"

"I have them. They make interesting viewing."

"You would be wise not to take copies."

"I assure you, I have better things to watch in my spare time."

"Good."

"So where do you want the exchange to take place?"

"I was thinking somewhere convenient for us both. We're quite close to Gatwick. I assume you are hiding out somewhere around Brighton. Do you want to make a suggestion?"

Powell was a little surprised Crawford was willing to let him choose a venue for the handover. He was probably trying to put Powell at ease, which he would have rightfully considered necessary after what happened at Leicester Square. It was also a touch of arrogance on Crawford's part.

Powell was under no illusion Crawford would simply shake hands and walk away, once they made the exchange. He was certain Crawford would spring some form of trap. He obviously felt confident of being able to do so whichever location they met. Given the resources he had at his disposal, his confidence wasn't really surprising.

Without Al-Hashimi and Barnes, plan A went down the drain. They would have none of the evidence the Director General needed before he was willing to act. He could copy the files but he doubted they would be enough to make the DG act? He needed to choose somewhere to meet where he had the advantage.

"Do you know the aptly named Devil's Dyke?" Powell asked. It was somewhere he knew like the back of his hand. He had been running there hundreds of times. The hills presented a formidable challenge but were perfect for Kickboxing training.

"No but I can look it up. Where is it?"

"Ten minutes from Brighton. It's a popular beauty spot with a great view. There's a car park at the top beside the pub. We can make the exchange there. Let's not pretend either of us is going to come alone. I will have two men with me as well as Al-Hashimi and Barnes. Make sure you only bring two men with you. You will need them because Al-Hashimi can't walk unaided after what you did to him."

"What time?"

"I need two hours to get there."

"So you aren't back in Brighton," Crawford said. It was a statement not a question.

Powell glanced at his watch. "We'll meet you there at Six."

He ended the call and turned to Brian. "Forget plan A or plan B, we need to come up with something new in the next two hours."

CHAPTER FIFTY THREE

Powell was the only person familiar with the location and had explained the layout and plan to the others. Brian drove up the narrow road leading to Devil's Dyke, followed a little way back by O'Neill, who was driving Powell's car. Powell had told Crawford he would have two men with him so was using O'Neill as an ace up his sleeve in case of trouble. That there would be some form of trouble Powell had little doubt.

Powell directed Brian not to park in the first car park by the pub but to drive past and park in the additional spaces past the pub. He had instructed O'Neill to park in the first car park, which was where he expected Crawford to park. There were plenty of other cars parked and quite a few people walking their dogs, buying ice creams from a van or just going for a drink in the pub. It was a renowned beauty spot and always busy with visitors

Powell stepped outside the car, telling the others to remain inside and surveyed the surrounding area. They were at the top and on one side of a very steep hill with commanding views of flat countryside, many miles into the distance. In front of them was the open, grass covered top of the hill where there was no place to hide. To his back but off to one side was the large pub.

There were a few bushes directly behind where he was standing but they afforded little cover for someone to hide and people were continually walking past. There could be some of Crawford's men hidden amongst those out for a walk but they were in full view of a great many others and Powell couldn't see them causing trouble somewhere so public.

Crawford would have studied the maps and be aware you could only reach the top by a single road. It was possible to walk up the Dyke itself but it was in open view and anyone trying to escape in that direction would make an easy target. Powell believed he had chosen a good location for the exchange.

Al-Hashmi was on the back seat with Jenkins and Barnes. Jenkins had his weapon aimed at both of them. Powell signalled to Brian for him to get out of the car.

"I'm going to go stand on the grass," Powell said. "I'll take Barnes with me so Crawford can identify us."

"You'll make an easy target," Brian pointed out.

"He needs Al-Hashimi even more than Barnes so I don't think he'll just shoot the two of us. At least I hope not." Powell managed a small smile.

"I'll cover you as best I can from here."

"Right, let's get Barnes out of the car and get on with this."

They returned to the car and Powell took Barnes by the arm as he pulled him from the back seat. He had his other hand inside his jacket pocket firmly gripping the handle of his gun. "No funny business," Powell warned. "I will have no compunction about shooting you dead if you do anything to try and sabotage this exchange."

"I'm sure you would and as I have spent far too much time in your company, I'm equally keen for the exchange to take place without incident."

"We're walking over there," Powell said, pointing to the middle of the open grass area. "There's no rush."

Barnes did as instructed and walked slowly.

"This is far enough," Powell said.

It was an area where at the weekend there would be many hang gliders jumping off the side of the hill. He had a good view towards the right where he expected to see Crawford emerge from the car park. To his left he could see Brian and behind him the car with Al-Hashimi inside.

Powell's phone rang and identified Afina as the caller.

"Where are you?" Crawford asked.

"In the middle of the grassy area opposite the car park. You can't miss me."

Crawford disconnected the call without further comment. A moment later Powell saw him standing on the side of the road looking in his direction. Powell saw Crawford raise the phone to his ear so wasn't surprised when his own phone rang again.

"Where's Al-Hashimi?" Crawford asked.

"Nearby. Where's Afina?"

"She's here. How do you want to do this?"

"First let me see Afina is with you."

Crawford looked back into the car park and gave a wave. After a minute two men appeared either side of Afina. She smiled when she recognised

Powell. It was enough to confirm she was okay.

"I'll get Al-Hashimi," Powell said. He waved at Brian to bring him forward.

It took a couple of minutes for Jenkins and Brian to get Al-Hashimi out of the car and join Powell.

"He can't walk by himself," Powell explained to Crawford. "Send one of your men over here. Then he can help Barnes to bring him back to you. As they start walking towards you, send Afina to me."

Powell watched as Crawford put the phone down and said something to one of the men, who then let go of Afina's arm and started walking across the road in Powell's direction. Powell stepped a pace away from the others so he could cover the man's approach.

"You are sending me back to them?" Al-Hashimi queried, his eyes showing panic. "You know they will kill me?"

"You are like gold to them and they intend to mine you for a long time to come. If you tell them what they want to know, I'm sure there will be no more torture."

"You are as bad as them," Al-Hashimi spat out.

"What do you want me to say? Do you want my sympathy? I'll save that for the innocent people you killed, who were enjoying a day out watching the marathon."

Al-Hashimi turned away and looked into the distance. "You are right... I was not always like I am today... I do not want your sympathy for myself but maybe for the hundreds of thousands of innocent people your government has murdered in Iraq. A few dozen from the West are killed and you act like it is the end of the world. Are our lives not equally as important?"

"The answer is not terrorism," Powell said emphatically.

"Your leaders are just as much terrorists. The only difference is they have more money and weapons. For every bomb we make you drop one hundred or more on us."

"We want to live in peace," Powell stressed.

"That is a lie. The West is engaged in a modern day crusade against Islam."

"Right now, I am concerned only about this exchange."

"This woman must be very important to you. Is she your wife?"

"No, she is more like my daughter."

"I understand. I would do the same in your place. I suppose I should be grateful. I didn't think I would ever again get to enjoy the countryside like this… Even though it has only been for a short time." He sucked the fresh air greedily into his lungs. Then he added, "My family were all killed by your bombs. I have nothing left to live for."

Powell had nothing further to say. He watched closely as Crawford's man arrived and silently took over Jenkins position supporting Al-Hashimi. Barnes then took the other arm from Brian.

"We're good to go," Powell said into the phone. "Let me have a quick word with Afina."

Crawford handed the phone to Afina but remained close enough to hear what was being said.

"Afina, when he tells you to start walking, just come towards me at a normal pace and everything will be fine. Don't try to run."

"Okay."

"Give the phone back now." Once Crawford had the phone again Powell continued, "Let's do it." He turned to Barnes and said, "You can go. Remember we are all armed and won't hesitate to shoot you if anything happens to Afina."

Barnes and the other man took the first few paces towards Crawford and at the same time Afina started walking. Powell watched carefully but was reasonable confident the exchange was going to take place without drama. However, he was also certain Crawford did not intend to simply let them drive away into the sunset and live happy ever after.

CHAPTER FIFTY FOUR

Powell ended the call to Crawford and watched until Afina had safely passed Al-Hashimi going in the other direction.

Powell quickly called O'Neill. "How's it look over there," he asked.

"Seems okay. I can't spot any other of Crawford's men. Whatever they're planning, I don't think it's imminent."

"Right, then it's time for you to leave. All being well, we'll see you in about fifteen minutes."

Powell ended the call and returned his attention to the exchange. Afina had increased her pace and was getting close. Al-Hashimi was moving slower, which was a positive. Every second's advantage might end up being important.

Out of the corner of his eye, Powell saw O'Neill drive out of the car park. He hoped he wasn't going to regret having sent him away too early.

Afina ignored Powell's instructions and ran the last few yards. She threw herself into Powell's arms.

"It's good to see you," she said. "I was so scared."

"We need to get going," Powell said, breaking away. "We aren't out of the woods yet."

He gave one last look in Crawford's direction to see Al-Hashimi delivered. Then they all headed towards the car where they were out of view of Crawford and his team.

"Follow me," Powell instructed, walking past the car and down a grassy incline.

He led them over the brow of the hill and before they disappeared completely from view, he glanced behind and was pleased he couldn't see any obvious sign of being followed. They walked at a fast pace down a steep hill but it was a walk he had done many times before and knew was safe. He had been pleased to see Afina was wearing trainers and not shoes with a heel.

They took paths that looked more suitable for mountain goats and were soon at the top of the Three Hundred Steps, which Powell knew led down towards the village of Poynings. He'd run up the steps many times as part of his kick boxing training. He was relieved to have reached cover. They could no longer be seen from above as there were trees overhanging the steps.

The fast pace didn't encourage anyone to speak and they were focused on not losing their footing. They were soon at the bottom of the steps and Powell was relieved to see O'Neill waiting for them, parked up at the side of the road.

Powell opened the rear door of the car and took a bag of clothes from the back seat. "Afina, can you please sit in the car and change all your clothes."

Afina looked as if she hadn't heard properly. "What did you say?"

"You must get rid of all your clothes urgently," Powell emphasised. "Crawford may have put a tracker on you. It doesn't even have to be a solid object nowadays. They can just use a powder." He thought it was unlikely as nobody had given chase, which they could have done if they had planted a tracker but it was best to be safe.

Afina did as asked. She sat on the backseat and a minute later emerged in different clothes. The men had all been gallant enough to look away while she changed. She handed the bag with her old clothes to Powell and he threw them into a nearby clump of bushes.

"Right, we need to hurry," Powell said. "O'Neill, you can keep driving. I'll sit in the front."

They all piled into the car and O'Neill accelerated away.

"This was a good move on your part," O'Neill said. "As I drove down the hill there were two cars waiting on the side of the road, who I would bet were Crawford's men."

"I'm not surprised. By now he's probably guessed we have other plans but he doesn't know what car we're driving."

"He wouldn't have to be a genius to guess it's your car," Jenkins said. "We should keep off the motorways so we stay away from the cameras. Otherwise they can find us too easily."

"I suppose you're right," Powell agreed. "I must be getting old. My brain's slowing down. I should have thought of that. Let's stick to the side roads."

"Can I borrow your phone," Afina asked Powell. "I need to call my mother to let her know I am okay."

"Of course," he said. "But make it very quick. Crawford may try and find us by our phones. We all have them switched off."

"I will just be one minute," Afina said, accepting Powell's phone.

Everyone could hear as Afina told her mother she was well and would call her again later.

"So what do we do next?" Brian asked, once Afina had finished her call and handed the phone back to Powell.

"I've been thinking about our options," Powell replied. "And I believe the best thing we can do is to publish what we know. If the whole world knows what we have discovered, then it makes it difficult for the likes of Crawford to come after us. The government and all the agencies, including the CIA, will be on the back foot."

"Publish and be damned," Brian agreed. "I will call the DG and let him know. I'm not sure he will be very happy about going public but at least we're giving him notice."

"Is your job at risk by us publishing?" Powell questioned.

"I don't think so," Brian replied. "I will say it's all your idea and I wasn't in favour but you went ahead anyway."

"That's probably for the best. We need you to keep us informed from the inside. If he acts fast, he may be still able to pick up Crawford and Barnes. Is the tracking device working?"

Brian checked his phone. "Working fine. He's heading back towards the A23. Where did you end up putting the tracker?"

"Tina wrapped it into the fresh bandage on Al-Hashimi's foot. Because he's in so much pain she doesn't think he will detect it."

"He may not be travelling with Crawford. There's a fair chance Crawford will have his men take him to a new safe house while he and Barnes head back to London."

"Who is Tina?" Afina suddenly asked. "And what is all this talk about publishing?"

"She's the sister of Samurai," Powell explained. "He is the hacker, who helped me trace where the Bennett children were living in Saudi Arabia. Do you remember?"

"Yes, I remember."

"He is going to publish our story on the internet. He is sending it to all the news outlets."

"You have been busy," Afina smiled.

"We have. Give me ten minutes and then I'll bring you up to date with everything that's happened while you were away."

Powell looked sideways to O'Neill. "Do you have the registration number of the car Crawford was driving?"

O'Neill recited the number out loud.

"I think we've done everything we can do. Let's hope the DG acts on it," Powell said.

"At the very least, the Home Secretary will find it difficult to block an investigation," Brian said.

"I'm sure he will try hard to block an investigation if he's implicated," Powell replied.

"There is also another important consideration," Jenkins added. "If Crawford is planning further terrorist attacks, as Barnes says, then he'd be a fool to go ahead with new attacks once the story comes out. I think publishing is the best way of stopping further attacks and that means we will be saving lives."

"We're all agreed then?" Powell asked.

Hearing no dissenting voices, he took out his phone and pushed the fast key for Samurai's number. "Go ahead and publish," Powell said. He felt a bit like he was launching an atomic weapon. The fallout would be similar. Whether the full extent of the conspiracy would ever be revealed he doubted.

"The information can be online within ten minutes," Samurai answered. "There will be no going back once I hit the send key."

"Go ahead. I'm not sure what exactly the outcome will be but it is our best option. It's our only option."

"A disruptive strategy is often the best approach. It works in technology. Information is a more powerful weapon than guns."

Powell hoped he was right. "Send me a text to confirm when it's live. And thanks for all your help."

"My pleasure. It should make for interesting headlines. I look forward to following the story from my home abroad. My friends will ensure it has global coverage."

"You have a home abroad?"

"My work has paid very well over the years. I have several homes. I intend to move to the sunshine for a period of time and let the dust settle. It means from tomorrow, I will be out of phone contact. If you need to get hold of me in an emergency, you must place an advert in the Argus personal ads. I will then contact you."

"What about Tina?"

"She enjoys the sun."

"Good luck and thanks again for your help."

Powell ended the call feeling a sense of relief. Samurai was no fool. He and Tina would be safer abroad. They had discussed the issue Barnes knew where they lived and Samurai had said not to worry but Powell had been concerned.

Powell was also feeling in need of spending some time abroad. He was feeling tired and wanted a holiday. He would take Afina to Rome or Venice perhaps. They were two of his favourite cities. He knew she had been to neither. There was little to celebrate but the two of them deserved a break. When they reached the hotel where they were going to spend the night, he would start searching the internet for flights. The bar could stay shut for a few more days.

EPILOGUE

The presentation was to take place at Buckingham Palace and Powell was surprised but pleased to receive an invitation. It was his first visit to the Palace and in all likelihood would be his last. Although he wouldn't get to meet the Queen in person, he would get to see her make the award.

He was sat with about twenty other guests, who had loved ones receiving a variety of awards. The recipients of the awards were sat in a special row of seats at the front. The room had thick carpet and the walls were covered in large portraits and ornate, gold decoration. Around the room were stood Yeoman of the Guard in their red and gold, Tudor style uniforms.

Powell had time to think about recent events while he waited for the ceremony to commence. It had been a traumatic six months for the British people. Samurai's release of a story speculating there was a conspiracy that went to the heart of government, enjoyed a short life in the media. The government quickly sent DA-Notices to all the mainstream media outlets citing implications for national security, which put an end to further articles.

It was left to the foreign press, especially in France and Germany, to freely publish their stories but much was just conjecture and speculation, and even these stories were soon replaced on the front pages by the reporting of further acts of terrorism around the world.

The official government reports identified Phoenix as responsible for the London pub bombing, in addition to the attacks in Brighton. There had been CCTV at the pub but on the night in question it had not been working. The truth was that one of the first people on the scene worked for a secret branch of MI6 and had swapped the tape showing Brown arriving and leaving, for one that was blank.

Al-Hashimi was reported as shot dead resisting arrest. The truth, Brian revealed, was that he was already dead when they found him, killed by a cocktail of drugs, which had been injected into his body soon after he was handed back to Crawford. His value had finally been outweighed by the risk of keeping him alive. Al-Hashimi was named as the marathon bomber and the press were informed all the terrorists responsible for the atrocities were accounted for and dead. It made for a better story than making wild accusations about political intrigue.

ISIS was blamed for all the attacks and the Prime Minister gave an impassioned speech from Downing Street, promising swift retaliation. Parliament passed an emergency Bill supporting additional air strikes in Syria, which took place within days. A further bill doubled spending on counter-terrorism.

Powell met with the DG and Brian where he was asked not to stir up more trouble. The DG promised that he and his counterparts in MI6 were routing out the bad apples. There was no appetite for public examination of possible conspiracy theories. That would only be playing into the hands of the terrorists.

Crawford had scurried back to America before he could be formally kicked out of the country. A very strong complaint had been made about his suspected behaviour and the CIA were left in no doubt he was persona non grata in the UK.

According to the DG, Barnes had been dealt with, whatever that truly meant. Powell suspected he had been pensioned off and he'd gone back to life in the country. A small price to pay compared with the price paid by Lara.

The only people who seemed to escape any censure were the politicians linked to Barnes and Crawford. The DG promised there would be an inquiry but there wouldn't be any washing of dirty linen in public.

The most positive outcome was that there were no further terrorist attacks. Whatever Crawford had been planning as his final attack never came to fruition. Six months on from the last attack, the country was returning to normal and the threat had receded in most people's minds.

Powell had wanted to be sure Afina and the rest of them were safe from any further attempts on their lives. The DG was able to assure him that was the case. So when the DG, on behalf of the establishment, asked Powell for his silence, he had only one demand in return for quietly returning to Brighton.

Today was the day the DG honoured Powell's demand. A large fanfare announced the event was about to commence. At each end of the room where Powell was sat, two pairs of ebony-veneered cabinets with gilt-bronze mounts were built into the wall beneath tall mirrors. The mirror and cabinet opened as one to reveal a concealed door and in walked the Queen attended by a number of men in suits. The room fell quiet and everyone stood while the Queen walked to the centre of the room and stood behind a small, raised dais. One of her staff then asked everyone to sit.

Powell watched as Lara's name was read out and her father walked forward to shake hands with the Queen and receive her posthumous George Cross medal, for an act of the most conspicuous courage, in circumstances of extreme danger. Her actions had saved the lives of many innocent bystanders.

The press had been fed the story she worked for MI6 and had been tracking Al-Hashimi's cell, when she was captured by the terrorists. They subsequently placed the suicide vest on her, drugged her and threw her out of a van in Leicester Square. She had quickly become a national heroine.

The George Cross being the highest gallantry award for civilians, Lara's father was a very proud man. Powell had spoken with him and explained how she had helped him in Saudi Arabia to recover the Bennett children. She was a friend and would be missed.

Powell initially felt some feelings of guilt. He had failed to protect Lara but the feelings had eroded over the months. It had been Lara's choice to work for MI6. She had chosen a dangerous career and he wasn't responsible for her death. At least he had managed to establish her innocence and she was truly deserving of her award. He would remember her fondly despite them having shared a rocky past.

THE END

TRAFFICKING
Powell Book 1

Trafficking is big business and those involved show no remorse, have no mercy, only a deadly intent to protect their income.

Afina is a young Romanian girl with high expectations when she arrives in Brighton but she has been tricked and there is no job, only a life as a sex slave.

Facing a desperate future, Afina tries to escape and a young female police officer, who comes to her aid, is stabbed.

Powell's life has been torn apart for the second time and he is determined to find the man responsible for his daughter's death.

Action, violence and sex abound in this taut thriller about one of today's worst crimes.

5* Reviews

"This book is not for the faint hearted but it is a brilliant read."

"Keeps you at the edge of your seat throughout."

"Exciting, terrifying, brilliant."

"One of the best books I have read in a long time!"

"Will leave you breathless."

ABDUCTED
Powell Book 2

Powell returns in an action packed novel of violence, sex and betrayal!

He is trying to recover two children from Saudi Arabia, who have been abducted by their father.

In a culture where women are second class citizens, a woman holds the key to the success or failure of his mission.

Meanwhile, back in Brighton, Afina is trying to deal with a new threat from Romanian gangsters.

From the streets of Brighton to Riyadh, Powell must take the law into his own hands, to help the innocent.

5* Reviews

" Trafficking was masterful and this one is even better."

"Great thriller."

"Fabulous twists and turns."

"Excellent read."

"Strong, interesting characters."

REVENGE.

There is no greater motivator for evil than a huge sense of injustice!

Tom Ashdown, an unlikely hero, owns a betting shop in Brighton and gambles with his life when he stumbles across an attempted kidnapping, which leaves him entangled in a dangerous chain of events involving the IRA, a sister seeking revenge for the death of her brother and an informer in MI5 with a secret in his past.

Revenge is a fast paced thriller, with twists and turns at every step.

In a thrilling and violent climax everyone is intent on some form of revenge.

5* Reviews

"Fast paced from the start and it only goes faster!"

"This novel is a real page turner!"

"It will keep you on the edge of your seat."

"Revenge is an example of everything that I look for in an action thriller."

ENCRYPTION.

In a small software engineering company in England, a game changing algorithm for encrypting data has been invented, which will have far reaching consequences for the fight against terrorism.

The Security Services of the UK, USA and China all want to control the new software.

The Financial Director has been murdered and his widow turns to her brother-in-law to help discover the truth. But he soon finds himself framed for his brother's murder.

When the full force of government is brought to bear on one family, they seem to face impossible odds. Is it an abuse of power or does the end justify the means?

Only one man can find the answers but he is being hunted by the same people he once called friends and colleagues.

5* Reviews

"A Great English Spy Thriller."

"This is a great story! Once I started reading it, I could not put it down."

"A superior read in a crowded genre!"

"Full of memorable characters and enough twists and turns to impress all diehard thriller junkies, it is a wonderful read"

"If you're a fan of Ludlum, and love descriptive prose like that of Michener, you'll be right at home."

ABOUT THE AUTHOR

Bill Ward lives in Brighton with his German partner Anja. He has retired from senior corporate roles in large IT companies and is now following a lifelong passion for writing! With 7 daughters, a son, stepson, 2 horses, a dog and 2 cats, life is always busy!

Bill's other great passion is supporting West Bromwich Albion, which he has been doing for more than 50 years!

Connect with Bill online:

Twitter: http://twitter.com/billward10bill

Facebook: http://facebook.com/billwardbooks